Quincy

"Wait!"

He stilled. "What is it?"

Holly lifted from the bedside, her legs shaking. "What about tonight? Our wedding night?"

He turned toward her again, his eyes charged with fierce resistance. "Do not assume our marriage is real, *wife*. It is in name alone. What you took of my body and put in that infernal painting is all you will *ever* take of me."

He stalked from the room, leaving the door ajar.

Holly blanched. She dropped backward, plopping onto the bed. She would *never* be with her husband? She would never run her fingers across his rolling muscles or feel the heat of his flesh beneath her hands? She would never taste his sensuous lips or hear his seductive voice in her ear, arousing her senses? She would never know the intimate feel of him inside her? Or have children? Ever?

Her heart ballooned. Her lungs expanded like storm clouds. To be leg shackled in matrimony without any of the sensual benefits was unrighteous. And Holly wouldn't stand for it. Her husband desired her, she knew it. And she *would* have him. All of him. Even if she had to seduce the stubborn rake.

ROMANCES BY **Alexandra Benedict**

The Hawkins Brothers Series
Mistress of Paradise
The Infamous Rogue
The Notorious Scoundrel
How to Seduce a Pirate

The Too/Westmore Brothers Series
Too Great a Temptation
Too Scandalous to Wed
Too Dangerous to Desire

The Fallen Ladies Society
The Princess and the Pauper

Stand Alone Romance
A Forbidden Love

AND COMING SOON
How to Steal a Pirate's Heart

ALEXANDRA BENEDICT

How To Seduce A Pirate

www.AlexandraBenedict.ca

For my readers,
who would not let me forget
about these dashing rogues.

Thank you for your support
and encouragement.

The Hawkins Family Tree

James Hawkins
(b. 1785)
The Infamous Rogue
and
Mistress of Paradise

William Hawkins
(b. 1787)
How to Steal a Pirate's Heart

Mirabelle Hawkins
(b. 1800)
Too Great a Temptation

Edmund Hawkins
(b. 1802)
The Notorious Scoundrel

Quincy Hawkins
(b. 1804)
How to Seduce a Pirate

How To Seduce A Pirate

PROLOGUE

London, 1826

As the snowfall thickened, Miss Holly Turner hastened her booted steps, finally reaching the front door at number twenty-seven. She rapped on the wood, glancing from side to side. The street was deserted on Christmas Eve. Still, her fingers trembled. If discovered at the notorious gaming hell, her reputation would be ruined. But she needed to take the dramatic measure. She wasn't in a position to make the unusual arrangements herself. She needed assistance. And the impervious Madam Barovski was *the* reputed hostess of the ton, capable of satisfying even the strangest request.

As soon as the barrier opened, Holly whisked inside the elegant townhouse. Her eyes darted toward the principal rooms. Empty. She sighed. She had insisted upon the utmost discretion, and Madam Barovski had vowed her patrons would be engaged in the upstairs bedrooms at such a late hour. Even so, Holly maintained her long cape and hood, concealing her identity.

"Good evening, Miss," greeted the older woman, her features a composition of unflinching banality.

"Good evening," murmured Holly. "Is everything prepared?"

"As you requested, Miss."

Upon the assurance, Holly reached inside her carpetbag and removed a draft, handing her hostess the agreed upon sum. The woman accepted the banknote, slipping it between her breasts.

"This way, Miss."

At the top of the stairs, Madam Barovski stopped and pointed down the hall. "Room nine."

And with those cursory words, the gaming mistress descended the spiral staircase and disappeared from sight.

Of course she wasn't going to accompany Holly. The less the woman witnessed the better. Still, Holly would've preferred a chaperone.

She looked down the darkened passageway, her heart pounding, and took a cautionary step. The floorboards blessedly didn't creak, and she quietly passed the other rooms, searching for number nine.

Holly winced when she heard the crack of a whip and a man groan in agony—or was it ecstasy? Skirting along, she soon arrived at the designated chamber.

The brass number glinted in the dim gaslight, and her heart boomed even harder. After a measured breath, she pressed the latch and pushed open the barrier.

The room was piping warm, rich in red tones and scintillating under firelight. Holly entered the forbidden world and set down her carpetbag, quickly shutting the door behind her. Feeling safe at last, she lowered her hood and gasped at the figure in the bed.

The young man rested on his stomach, his muscular arms wrapped around a white pillow. The chamber was heavy with candles, and she watched the flickering glow play across his naked spine. Her eyes travelled to the small of his back and the slight curvature of his firm buttocks, but she saw no more of his nakedness, his lower body covered by a linen sheet.

Heavens, he was beautiful. More beautiful than Holly had imagined. A pulsing sensation drummed through her, her nerves tingling with unexpected life. She had never been so aware of her own skin, gooseflesh spreading across her limbs in prickling arousal.

Her breath quickened as she lifted her gaze to the man's handsome features. A curl of sable black hair dangled over his smooth brow. She noticed just a shadow of facial hair caressing his jaw and chin. His lips, so lush, whirred as he breathed deep and steady, fast asleep.

Soon she detected the sweet scent of opium in the room. He had indulged in the smoke. Was he nervous, like her? Nonsense, she thought. He was accustomed to such services. She was the novice here. And she had best get to work. She hadn't much time before dawn.

After another thorough assessment of his robust physique, her eyes returned to his slumbering face — and she found him alert.

Holly started at the pair of smoldering blue eyes

fixed on her. He studied her in the same sensational manner, moving his gaze down the length of her body and back up to her eyes, making her shudder with unwanted delight.

"What's your name, lass?"

His voice, thick and sensual, peeled away her inhibitions, and her breath hitched before she whispered, "Holly." Surely there was no harm in revealing her first name. She would never see him again after tonight.

A smile played in his eyes. "My very own Holly for Christmas. Madam is most generous."

Holly sensed trouble. His flirtation had a disarming affect on her, dashed her concentration. She had to grapple with her own tongue to set him back in his place.

"She is indeed," affirmed Holly. After all, her hostess *had* procured an outstanding masculine specimen. There was no contention there. "But I'm not here for your pleasure. You are here for mine."

He chuckled, a low rumble, and she found the sound a disturbing pleasure.

"Very well, Holly. How would you like me?"

"Just as you are."

His position was perfect, in truth. She picked up her carpetbag and crossed the room, settling in an armchair beside the hearth.

"You can hardly touch me from over there, sweet."

Heavens, he was going to make the experience a thorny one with his wicked words. "I've no intention of touching you."

He frowned. "Then what do you intend to do

4

with me?"

"Sketch you, of course. Now keep still."

Holly removed her sketch book and charcoal pencil and started working on his form. Her first male nude! She had only ever painted the female body. But this . . . this had to be worth the risk.

"Listen, sweet, if you're not going to have a bit of real fun, then get out so I can sleep."

She furrowed her brow. "I've paid good money for your time *and* silence."

The impudent rake. Hadn't Madam told him about her strict request? *No* conversation!

"What the devil are you talking about?" he snapped.

He started to rise from his drowsy slumber.

"Get back into the bed," she ordered, her voice cracking with panic.

But he stood up, naked, fully erect, glorious — and frightening beyond words. Holly dropped her jaw. *Heavens!*

He growled, "*You* paid for *me*?"

Holly blinked, then grabbed her belongings, sensing something was *very* amiss. "Madam said—"

"That witch is *selling* me?"

He took a thunderous step toward her.

With a shriek, Holly bolted from the room, the number nine swinging on the door as she dashed away. And it was in that moment she realized the number nine was *not* the number nine, but the number six upside-down. A nail must have come loose and fallen to the ground, the six swinging down to look like a nine.

Oh, no! She had made a horrible blunder. And

someone had seen her! Not the paid prostitute she'd hired, but *another* man.

Holly rushed pell-mell out of the gaming hell.

CHAPTER 1

London, 1827

Quincy Hawkins lathered a scone with butter and jam. As the last of his brothers to rise, he was breaking his fast alone in the dining parlor. He preferred the solitude. He wasn't sure when the strife with his older siblings had started, but their tedious reproofs of him had grown tiresome of late.

After devouring the scone, Quincy reached across the table for the morning broadsheet and quirked an amused brow at the sensational headline: *Lord H Crosses the Line of Decency!*

The Lord Byron of the painted world, Lord H produced erotic art, his work exhibited underground, showing only in illicit establishments and selling for neat sums. No one knew the artist's true identity, though he was rumored to live in France.

Quincy had seen a few of the man's pieces go up for auction, though he personally thought them rather tawdry, lacking any real sensuality; the sort of work a sexually inexperienced buck might find provocative. Certainly unworthy of all the public fuss.

But it seemed an indecency law had been broken. His middle brother, Edmund, a Bow Street Runner, was actually on the hunt for the elusive artist and his so-called scandalous work. Again, Quincy didn't understand the hullabaloo over naked breasts. He certainly adored them, but they weren't entirely hidden from society. The antiquity department at the British Museum was full of much lovelier nymphs.

As he bit into a second pastry, the butler entered the room, carrying a large silver tray stacked with gobs of letters. A hundred, at least! The servant set down the curious missives, most tied with ribbon and sprayed with heady perfume. Gads, the smell!

"What the devil's going on, Benson?" he mumbled, mouth full of jam and bread.

"This morning's post, sir."

A ridiculous amount of mail, thought Quincy. And why had Benson delivered it to the dining parlor and not the study?

"Well, pass it along to William. You know he takes care of the family's affairs."

His older brother, William, governed the bachelor roost since their eldest brother, James, had married and moved to Mayfair.

"They are all addressed to you, sir."

Quincy balked.

As the unflappable butler left the room, Quincy licked his fingers before he flipped through the monstrous piles of letters. There was no mistaking what Benson had said—every letter was addressed to him.

"What's all this, pup?"

Captain William Hawkins entered the dining parlor, a deep frown etched across his brow. He had the same intimidating height and muscular build as each of his brothers, but unlike the rest of the tempestuous brood, he was the most sensible of the lot. Truly, Quincy had never seen him lose his temper.

"I'm as confounded as you, old man."

His brother's frown darkened at the epithet. William had just turned forty years of age. And if Quincy was still the "pup" at age twenty-three, then his sibling was deservedly the "old man."

Quincy snatched a couple of letters, tearing off the frilly ribbons and breaking the wax seals. Skimming the feminine penmanship, he discovered a series of lusty proposals: some asked for a private dance at the next ball, others invited him to a secret rendezvous, and others still suggested an outright affair.

An irrepressible grin tugged at his lips. "It seems my sexual prowess is gaining acclaim."

William scowled.

Funning aside, Quincy *was* bewildered. What had happened to warrant the hoard of sexual offers?

William assumed a seat at the opposite end of the table and crossed his arms. "Well, if your 'sexual prowess' isn't taking up too much of your time, I want to know if you're prepared for our upcoming journey?"

After a long hiatus, he and William were scheduled to set sail in less than a week and resume their duties as privateers in the Royal Navy's African Squadron.

A year ago, William had been shot aboard ship, chasing a British slaver. The bullet to the chest had almost killed him, and it'd taken him near a year to recover and regain his strength.

"I'm prepared," said Quincy. "I even purchased a new monaural stethoscope along with a few more books on anatomy — in case you get shot again."

At the gibe, William's usually staid features twisted in what resembled fury. For a man who controlled his emotions at all times, it was a remarkable sight.

But it still riled Quincy, his absence aboard the *Nemesis* that day. If he had been there, he would have treated his brother's wound with the surgical skills he'd amassed over the years, and William would not have been butchered by the inexperienced tars aboard ship. His brother would have healed sooner. And he damn well wouldn't have come so close to death. But Quincy had been banned from that tour, accused of being too "ill," too attached to opiates to serve on a ship.

His brother just didn't appreciate the poppy and its healing effects. Quincy had once had trouble with the drug, taking too much at one time. But he knew better now. In properly measured doses, the compounded paste cured almost every ail, including insomnia — and crippling nightmares.

William studied him with a dubious expression, perhaps pondering if Quincy was capable of making the Atlantic crossing. But after a year on land, Quincy was restless with the desire to return to sea.

He was joining the tour—even if he had to stow away.

He was needed, too. He wouldn't let another slaver take aim at William or the rest of the crew. How could his galling brother forget Quincy had been reared on a schooner since he *was* a pup? He lived and breathed the life of a seaman. And while he might be the youngest of his brethren, he'd experienced as many battles and storms and near hangings as any of them.

A series of offbeat thumps resounded in the passageway. Someone carried a cumbersome object and was bumping into every piece of furniture along the way.

Soon his brother Edmund appeared, his arms outstretched as he maneuvered a massive canvas draped in red velvet. He dumped the painting on the ground, leaning it against the wall.

"What is that?" asked William, his black brows pinched together.

A breathless Edmund combed a hand through his mussed hair. "The most recent painting by Lord H."

"The erotic artist?" William exchanged bemused glances with Quincy. "Shouldn't you surrender it to the magistrate?"

"Hell, no!"

Quincy chuckled. "Turning pirate again, are you?"

For ten years, the Hawkins brothers had sailed the high seas as pirates. But after their beloved sister had married a duke, the four had retired their marauding ways and settled into the routine existences of respectable gentlemen.

"I didn't steal it," returned a surly Edmund. "I bought it."

He fished out a scrap of paper from his great coat pocket and handed William the bill.

"Blimey! This costs more than the house." As William's face turned a burning red, he demanded, "Why the hell did you buy it?"

"Because of this."

Edmund seized the velvet drape and tore it off the canvas.

They all three stared at Quincy's naked arse.

William first recovered from the blow, groaning and slumping his face in his palm. "You posed *nude*? How could you do this, Quincy?"

Quincy remained rigid, glaring at the wretched oil. It was him, all right, stretched out across a bed, naked, a white sheet covering his legs and only a small part of his arse.

But how? When? *Who* had painted it?

"I couldn't confiscate the painting without also turning it over to the authorities," said Edmund, "so I bought it and told the magistrate it'd sold before I could apprehend it."

"Did you have to pay a bleedin' fortune?" from an aghast William.

"I didn't have a choice. There was a frenzy of bidding, and I had to get the pup's arse out of public view."

Quincy would otherwise be flattered at the "frenzy of bidding" for his naked arse, but not under the circumstances. He finally marshaled his limbs into movement and approached the oil, analyzing the background. Dark red curtains. A fireplace near the foot of the bed. Candles. There was something gut wrenchingly familiar about the scenery, and he shut his eyes for a moment, groping through his hazy reflections.

"I can't keep hauling you out of scrapes, Quincy."

He turned toward Edmund, his muscles hardening. "Who bloody well asked you to be my keeper?"

Edmund scrunched his fists. "You clearly can't take care of yourself. The opium's completely smoked your brain."

"Damn it, I didn't pose for that!" cried Quincy, pointing at the oil. "I've never even met Lord bloody H."

As he studied the brush strokes in greater detail, a memory surfaced of a smoky bedroom alight with candles, a warm bed on a winter's eve and . . . a woman. No, he thought, flustered. Impossible.

"Enough." William stepped between them, arms outstretched. "Keep your heads. Both of you."

Quincy's heart hammered. He grabbed his pulsing skull as he remembered a vixen with strawberry-flaxen hair, light green eyes and pink, kissable lips.

He remembered more and more the night he had first met her, her cheeks flushed with heat, her breath rampant with arousal. He'd hardened at her sinful innocence, her obvious want. He'd thought her a comely wench come to pleasure him. But she had come for her own pleasure . . . with her sketch book.

Bullocks.

"Did you even think of Belle?" charged Edmund.

"And what this would do to her reputation?"

Quincy would never hurt his sister, Mirabelle, the Duchess of Wembury. He would sooner cut his own throat than cause her any pain.

He stepped away from the miserable artwork. His brothers glowered at him with obvious condemnation, now convinced he really was the irresponsible, skirt chasing, opium fiend in need of a keeper.

"At least we have the painting." Edmund sighed. "It's over."

"Have you seen this morning's post?" William gestured toward the reeking piles of perfumed letters. "You weren't the only one who recognized Quincy in the painting. Word of his 'sexual prowess' has traveled fast."

Quincy fisted his palms. He was going to kill *Lord H*.

CHAPTER 2

The Honorable Miss Holly Turner stepped into the ballroom wearing a burnished gown of gold taffeta, her locks pinned and curled in an elegant crown around her head and garnished with a ruby comb.

It had been seven years since she'd entered the glittering world of high society. A selfish part of her hoped she had not been forgotten. During her first season, she'd held the eye of every eligible bachelor, and she'd adored the flattering attention. But the scandal that had ravaged her father had forced her into seclusion, and her youthful heyday had passed.

With the passing of time, though, the gossip had also died. And now there was hope for her younger sister, Emma, to make a respectable match.

Holly looked over at her seventeen-year-old sister, adorned in white and wide-eyed as a dove. She felt the girl's fingers digging into her arm and smiled.

"Don't fret, love. You'll be the toast of the town."

Emma simpered. "I'm sure I'll forget every etiquette lesson, every dance step. Oh, Holly! What if no one asks me to dance?"

"Hush, Emma. Your dance card will be filled. Soon you'll need another and another still. Don't let your nerves spoil your wonderful evening. Look. Here comes our hostess."

The Countess of Brimsby approached the ladies with a broad smile. She had invited the sisters to her annual spring ball at Holly's behest and in honor of their late mother, her once cherished friend.

"Holly, my dear." The matron cupped her shoulders and kissed her on each cheek, officially marking her re-entrance into society. "You are as lovely as your mother."

"Thank you, Lady Brimsby."

"And you, Emma, how tall you've grown."

Emma offered a very presentable curtsy.

"Well done, my dear. Why, you'll have every young beau at your command, just as your sister once had."

Holly winced. Lady Brimsby had not said anything untruthful; Holly wasn't the freshest bloom in the garden anymore. Still, the unwitting remark stung worse than a bee.

"Come, girls, let me introduce you to all the eligible men."

It wasn't long before Holly's prediction had come true. Emma attracted the notice of many well-to-do gentlemen, and her dance card indeed overflowed with handsome suitors. She spent most of the night twirling across the dance floor, much to Holly's relief.

Holly herself received a few charming glances but quelled the impulse to encourage the courtiers. She was Emma's chaperone. And while Holly would love to dance, she needed to keep a close watch over her vulnerable sister.

As the night wore on, the air stifled. Holly couldn't step outdoors to escape the crush, not even for a moment, too afraid to leave her sister unattended. Instead, she headed toward the refreshment table and collected a glass of iced water. Just holding the chilled glass between her hands doused some of the stuffiness in the room.

"Might I have the next dance?"

She stiffened. Her heart pumped faster at the sound of that seductive male voice. She would never forget that voice. She had heard it even in her dreams.

There was really nowhere for her to hide, much less run. She was trapped. And she didn't want to imagine what awaited her if she confronted that voice—and the man it belonged to.

But she couldn't stand with her back to him either. The warmth from his body heated her spine, and she shivered with dread. How had he found her? Would he out her at the ball? In front of the ton? On her sister's important night? Heavens! Could she prevent another scandal in any way?

Wait! She was imagining the worst possible scenario. Perhaps he didn't recognize her? Perhaps he just wanted to dance with an eligible lady? He had been asleep and drowsy with opium on the night she'd first met him. How much could he truly remember about her?

But what was he doing at the ball? Was he gentry? No. No. She'd made inquiries into his mysterious identity. He was not a lord, she was sure. And yet . . .

Her mind swirled with a thousand thoughts. It was time to learn the truth.

Hand shaking, she set down the iced water, hauled in a deep breath, then turned with a polite smile.

Her heart slammed against her chest as a pair of livid blue eyes penetrated her soul. Heavens, his eyes. The bluest blue. She had never seen him in full light and hadn't realized just how black his wavy hair was or how finely sculpted his features were without the trace of a beard. And tall. Ever so tall. With the same wide, muscular shoulders any artist would beg to study—or any lover would beg to touch.

Holly sensed her temperature rising, her throat growing parch. Strangely, the brilliant light from the ballroom detracted from his bewitching physique. He was still as sinfully handsome as she remembered—even when steaming mad—but he was a man to be admired under candlelight, in the shadows, in the time between dusk and dawn.

"I don't believe we've met," she said, voice strangled. She lifted her gloved hand for a customary buss on the knuckles. "The Honorable Miss Holly Turner."

His touch was both tender and strong, and she felt an involuntary spasm in her belly—and heard warning bells in her ears.

"I believe we've met before, Miss Turner."

At his husky voice, she shuddered. The man still possessed the same disarming affect on her with his low timbre. And when his sensuous lips caressed her hand, scorching her flesh right through the satin fabric, unbidden pleasure skittered down her spine.

"In fact," he whispered in a throaty vein, "I believe we know each other very well."

Holly's heart pounded ever harder. How much could she deflect as nonsense, the misconceptions of a half asleep, intoxicated man?

He murmured, "Intimately well."

A heady memory welled to the forefront of her thoughts—a naked man towering above her. So strong. So virile. So erect.

She was blushing, she knew. She couldn't restrain her body's response to his both charismatic and dangerous presence. Worse, curious eyes were turning toward them. Why? Was it really so unthinkable Holly might attract a suitor? She might be a spinster, but she was only five-and-twenty, hardly an old maid. And no one knew her identity as Lord H. Or that she had painted the stranger in front of her. So why all the nosy stares?

Holly could feel an anxious pressure on her throat. She mustered her bravado. She had to protect her sister. She had to disentangle herself from the Adonis before gossip spread. "I'm afraid you are mistaken, sir."

She tried to pull her hand away. His grip tightened.

"I think not, sweet."

Oh, no! He had called her that on the night they'd first met. He *did* remember the details of their brief encounter. How many, though?

"Shall we dance?"

Flustered, she croaked, "I'm not inclined to dance."

"A shame."

He escorted her onto the dance floor, maintaining an unbreakable hold of her hand. If she struggled, she'd receive even more intrusive attention from the onlookers. Heavens, requital had come!

He wrapped a muscular arm around her waist, holding her close, much too close. His fingers spread across her backside in a guarded embrace, and for a moment her memory slipped into the faraway past.

She found herself a debutant again in the arms of the season's most sought-after beau. All the mooning, coy, flirtatious winks of the feminine sex failed to attract his notice. He had eyes solely for her. She alone was worthy of his passionate attention.

In smooth steps, he guided her in a graceful waltz.

"Might I assume I paid for that dress and those jewels with the fortune I forked up to retrieve my naked arse?"

Holly gasped at his outright, crude language in the *middle* of the dance floor. Her foolish reverie shattered as she desperately searched her immediate surroundings. Had anyone overheard the exchange? But his voice had been low enough to disappoint the eavesdroppers. Couples strained their ears toward them, but none expressed shock at his outrageous inquiry.

"Sir, I—"

"Quincy," he interrupted. "Quincy Hawkins."

His name jarred her to the bone. She had preferred to think of him as a dream. But he was real.

And he posed a very real threat to her newfound position in society. She needed to know as much about him as possible, to appease him, to take the hellfire out of his eyes.

He was rich, she reflected, wearing the most fashionable togs. And he had enough money to purchase her — his? — painting. But he'd mentioned no title. A boon, there. She was unfamiliar with his family name. And yet, she'd been absent from society for so long. He might be the latest young buck on parade. He appeared a couple of years her junior. She had likely missed his entrance into society. He had probably arrived shortly after her departure.

But she had been *so* sure he wasn't a gentleman. Her subtle inquiries into his identity had confirmed him a sailor. A sailor! Her source had clearly lied to her.

"Mr. Hawkins, you are a gentleman, and I —"

"I'm not a true gentleman, Miss Turner. I only pretend to be one for the sake of my sister."

"Your sister?"

"The Duchess of Wembury."

Holly groaned.

"And you, Miss Turner, have embarrassed my sister with your infernal artwork."

Worse and worse. A rake might be flattered by the amorous attention he'd received from the painting, but a rake protecting his sister? His *duchess*-of-a-sister?

Holly was doomed. She recognized his sister's title. Her husband, the Duke of Wembury, had been known as the "Duke of Rogues" in Holly's time. If nothing had changed in all these years, Holly had just embroiled herself with one of the most wicked family's in England!

Suddenly all the obtrusive stares made dreadful sense. Holly was dancing with the man in *the* painting — the painting that had all but abased the Duchess of Wembury.

Lightheaded, Holly grasped Mr. Hawkins in a firmer hold. Oh, why had she auctioned the painting of him? Why had she *ever* painted him in the first place?

It had never been her intent to do either, not after she'd realized her error in mixing up the rooms at the gaming hell. But his image had haunted her. And after several restless weeks, she'd expressed his likeness on canvas, hoping to release herself from his inexplicable hold.

But unleashing her creativity had only made him more desirable. Mr. Hawkins possessed an enigmatic allure. Soul. Mystery. And a story. *Who am I?* he had called from the canvas. *Come closer and find out . . .*

He had captured her breath. And she'd reasoned he'd capture the breaths of others as well — wealthy others. She'd been right on that count. The sum his likeness had fetched had finally provided her with the means she'd needed to launch her sister into society and provide her with a respectable dowry.

Now, Holly might lose everything on that gamble.

"Mr. Hawkins, there's been a terrible misunderstanding."

"I think not, *Lord H.*"

Again she looked to see if anyone had overheard

him. Thankfully, no.

"How did you discover me?" she whispered. If he had learned of her clandestine identity, might others discover it as well?

"A very forthcoming Madam Barovski."

"No, she would never reveal such a secret. Her reputation would be ruined. And trust, once lost, is irrecoverable. She'd lose all her patrons."

"Very astute, Miss Turner. But what if I had a brother, say a Bow Street Runner, who threatened to bring down her entire establishment if she didn't reveal the wench who'd come into my room on Christmas Eve?"

Holly scowled at the word "wench." Her paintings had sustained her and her sister in times of poverty. No one wanted art from a woman, much less serious art, and so she'd painted nudes incognito, resorting to disreputable tactics, like hiring prostitutes as models. It infuriated her to be considered a "wench" for the work she'd performed to survive.

"And might Madam Barovski betray one client to save all the others?" he murmured.

"She might, indeed," grumbled Holly, silently cursing Madam Barovski. And then an idea struck her. "Aren't you being a hypocrite, Mr. Hawkins?"

"I beg your pardon?"

"I paid for your services. You might have changed your mind about posing for me when you chased me from the room, but that's no reason to upbraid me or intimidate me with exposure. If you didn't want the attention, you should not have agreed to the transaction."

His features darkened like thunderclouds. Perhaps she had crossed a line with her flippant response. But she was already up to her neck in boiling water.

"Have you lost your mind?" he growled, eyes flashing. "*I* pose for you?"

"I hired a male model to draw. And Madam Barovski directed me to your room."

"She directed you to another room. You sneaked into mine."

Holly widened her features in her best imitation of horror. "You are *not* the model I hired? Oh, Mr. Hawkins, I am ever so regretful." She was sorry. Very sorry, indeed. "Cleary there has been a grave mistake."

"I don't give a damn about your mistake or apology, Miss Turner. But if you ever produce another painting with my likeness, you will regret it."

At that moment, the music ended and her cantankerous partner escorted her off the dance floor. Without another glance, he turned and stalked away.

Abandoned at the refreshment table, all eyes pinned on her, Holly sensed that familiar strangulation at her throat.

Where had Mr. Hawkins left her? Figuratively, of course. Would he reveal her notorious identity in revenge? Would his brother, the Bow Street Runner, apprehend her for breaking an indecency law?

She was well aware of the chances she took each time she presented and sold a nude. What would become of her now? Her poor sister?

Holly couldn't allow matters to rest on such unstable ground. After checking to make sure her sister was safe, she withdrew from public scrutiny and quickly skulked after Mr. Hawkins.

CHAPTER 3

Quincy stormed from the ballroom. He'd never been so infuriated with anyone in all his years, especially a woman. He adored the fairer sex. Hell, he'd charmed and seduced them since he was thirteen.

But Miss Holly Turner provoked him beyond measure. He fisted his palms to contain his fury — and his lust. He couldn't believe how hard he was for the conniving wench. He had never wanted to both throttle *and* bed a woman. And the opposite passions wrecked havoc on his innards.

He reached his coach and entered the parked vehicle. He had told the driver to wait for him at the front entrance, for he'd no intention of staying at the ball. He'd achieved his purpose: to put a stop to any more illicit art featuring his arse.

As he proceeded to close the door, lithe fingers wedged between the frame and he almost crushed the appendages.

"Ouch!" cried a feminine voice.

"Bloody hell."

He pushed opened the door and found Miss

Turner massaging her hand. Without another thought, he grabbed her wrist and hauled her into the coach, slamming the door.

"What the devil is the matter with you?" he demanded.

"I need to speak with you in private," she said, taking the opposite squab.

"And if you'd been seen?"

"I took care no one was spying. We *must* talk."

The desperation in her voice cooled some of his temper, but none of his lust. The gas lighting from the street seeped into the carriage and rested across her face, bathing her fair skin and elfin features in a hazy glow. She had a pure and innocent beauty, like an unspoiled country girl. Even her gown and jewels couldn't take away her earthly charm, and he found himself captivated by her soft sweetness. How could such a fair, unassuming creature be the infamous Lord H?

His blood burned to have her alone in the vehicle, and the impulse to hold her again overwhelmed him. As she continued kneading her fingers, he took her injured hand in his. She gasped. He ignored her protest and slowly removed one glove, stroking her slender fingers from joints to phalanxes, palpating for fractures. How could such fine, dainty fingers create such sinful art?

He arched her hand toward the window, illuminating her polished nails. Not a speck of paint stained her flesh. And yet she had painted him. She had seen him for no more than two minutes, but she had memorized his features, his muscles, his arse in wretchedly suburb detail.

The blood in his veins burned hotter. Miss Holly Turner had seen him in the raw. Rather unfair he'd not had the same pleasure.

"Ahem."

The moment she cleared her throat, he released her hand.

"The bones are not broken," he said.

She quickly stuffed her hand back inside her glove. "I'm pleased to hear that."

"But your fingers will be sore for a few days." He crossed his arms over his chest and leaned against the squab, resisting the temptation to touch her again. He was bloody daft. "What are you doing here, Miss Turner?"

"I would like your assurance, Mr. Hawkins, that you will not reveal my identity as Lord H."

"And why should I give you such assurance after the trouble you've caused my family?"

"I made a mistake. I truly believed I had entered the room of my hired model. I—" She hesitated, as if she'd more to confess, then resumed, "I have a sister, Mr. Hawkins. She is only seventeen and tonight is her debut in society. I don't want scandal to ruin her chances of making a respectable match."

"Touché."

"I regret the embarrassment I caused your own sister. Truly, I do. Oh, Mr. Hawkins, surely you can understand my motivations? Wouldn't you do anything to protect your sister?"

He would, indeed. And he sensed the woman's manipulation. But he had no counterargument. He had already sacrificed his former way of life to safeguard his sister's reputation. He could not reproach Miss Turner for doing the same.

"I paint to support myself and Emma," she said. "I'm not a heartless wench, as you might suspect. I intended no harm with the painting."

He studied her from across the seat, her wide eyes and lovely full lips. There was naivety there, as well as sensuality. Cleverness. Even cunning. How had she found herself in this predicament? From what he'd gleamed, she was an orphan. Her late father a viscount. Had he squandered the family fortune, leaving her penniless?

Even more pressing, what was she hiding from him? She had hesitated a moment ago about her "mistake." But how had she entered the wrong bedroom at the gaming hell?

"How did you come to my room, Miss Turner?"

"I—I was told to go to room nine. You were in room nine."

"I was in room six."

She flushed.

"You cannot read, Miss Turner?"

"Of course I can I read," she shot, indignant. "The number was upside-down."

He rasped, "What?"

"I think, I mean." She scrunched her dress between her fists. "I think the number was upside-down."

"You *knew* you were in the wrong room?"

"No, I swear . . . Not at first."

Quincy heard his pulse pounding in his ears. "How could you make the work public? What if I was married? Or a politician? Or a bleedin' duke?"

"I would never be so reckless, so indifferent. I

believed you a sailor, that no one in society would ever recognize you."

"A heartless wench, indeed."

"No." She thumped her fist in her palm, then winced. "It was a mistake. An accident."

"A fortuitous accident for you, Miss Turner. A grave one for me. Get out."

"What?" she whispered.

"Get out of my coach."

"But this isn't my fault."

"It's mine, I suppose?"

Her trembling fingers went to her temples, rubbing them in circular motions. "This is all getting away from me."

"Aye, your charade is unraveling."

"I came to propose a truce.

"Bully to that," he snapped. "Why are you still in my coach?"

"Oh, deuces! This would not have happened if you weren't so unnaturally beautiful."

He stiffened. "I beg your pardon?"

Her hands went to her gaping mouth, but then she curled her fingers and fixed her eyes on him with plain heat. "What am I, an artist, to do when confronted with the perfect male subject? Walk away?"

Quincy stared at her, incredulous. She was actually blaming *him* for the disaster, the shifty wench. She wanted to study him, did she? She thought him the perfect male subject?

"Well, Miss Turner, far be it from me to stand in the way of your artistic pursuits." He plucked her from the opposite squab, saddling her in his lap.

"Take your hands, your eyes . . . your lips and study me until you're satisfied."

He brought her flushed mouth down over his. Her seductive lips opened, and she damn well took him up on his offer, raking her fingers through his hair and circling his throat, devouring him.

Blimey, she was insatiable. The harder he kissed her, the harder she kissed him in return. He had never met a woman with such unrestrained passion, and a flame ignited in his soul. An unfamiliar flame. Lust, aye. But something more. A need. A need for... He wasn't sure. He had no word for the curious sentiment. A part of him reached toward the peculiar light. Another part warned him to steer clear of it, that it would burn him alive.

Quincy wrenched away from her, struggling for air. His muscles trembled. Where the hell had all his senses gone? "I accept your truce."

She voiced hoarsely, "What?"

With great effort, he returned her to the opposite squab, his heart ramming against his chest like a raging bull caged in a stall.

"I will not reveal your identity as Lord H."

"Oh."

She gathered her own rampant breath and thumbed her loose hair behind her ears. Her disenchanted expression made him want her even more. It was madness.

Sweet madness.

Quincy opened the coach door. "Goodnight, Miss Turner."

Her first step quivered before she regained her bearing and descended the vehicle, murmuring,

"Goodnight."

As soon as she cleared the door, he slammed it closed and hammered on the roof, the driver taking off at breakneck speed.

CHAPTER 4

W hat am I to do?" She traced the contour of his cheek bone, her fingertips slipping over his chin and down the center of his throat. She murmured, "So unnaturally beautiful," before she took his lips into her wicked mouth — and he let her.

He weaved his fingers through her lush, unruly red hair and cupped the back of her head, holding her tight, pressing her more firmly against his body. Heaven, he thought. Pure heaven.

His muscles hardened at the salacious thrusts of her mouth, at her intimate exploration of his lips. He opened for her and welcomed her probing tongue with the excitement of a virginal youth, trembling with green want.

How could she do this to him?

How could she take him back to a time when he'd no experience with women? And she an innocent herself? But somehow she had opened a door long closed to him. And he walked through it with renewed hope . . .

A fist jabbed him in the shoulder.

"Wake up, pup."

Quincy grunted as the enchantment shattered and he found himself back in his bedroom, nursing a superb headache. He had taken opium paste in the form of sugar coated capsules to suppress his hellish nightmares; to forget every secret he had to keep and every reputation he had to protect; to forget the profound desire he had for one impudent wench.

To forget himself.

Slowly he rolled to the side of the bed and sat on the edge, elbows on his knees, a blanket covering his groin. He always slept in the nude.

William stood over him, arms akimbo.

"What the hell do you want, Will?"

"What happened at the ball last night?"

Raking his fingers through his mussed hair, Quincy yawned. "I confronted Lord H. She won't be making any more portraits of me."

"Anything else?"

Quincy focused his bleary eyes on his brother, the man's tight expression indicating he was waiting for more news. "No. Nothing else."

"*Lord H* didn't stumble from a coach with the Hawkins family crest, her hair askew, her face flushed?"

"Shit."

Quincy slumped his face in his hands. She had been seen. The wench had been seen — with him.

"You really have no self control."

At the condemnation in his brother's voice, Quincy stiffened. To be denounced for an affair without the fun of actually having one was unrighteous. "She came to *me*."

"Aye, I know. All women throw themselves at your feet. How can you resist any of them?"

Damn Holly! She'd had the audacity to blame him

for the painting's creation, and now she'd botched every other area of his life, for even under the opium's sedate effects, Quincy knew where the conversation with his brother would end—with his doom.

"The duke's gone off to obtain a special license. We sail in three days, so the wedding will be the day after tomorrow—unless you're resigning your post aboard the *Nemesis*?"

"No!"

"Fine. The day after tomorrow it is. It will be a simple affair, family only, no fancy wedding clothes. A church ceremony. A wedding lunch. And it's over."

Over, indeed. "Will, I can't—"

"Aye, you can. And you will. Do you understand what you've done? Miss Turner is the daughter of a late viscount. She is gentry. You will make this right, even if I have to plant a pistol in your back and stand behind you at the altar."

"She did this," hissed Quincy. "She did this on purpose to trap me into marriage."

A poor viscount's daughter with a younger sister in need of a wealthy match. Wouldn't it be grand if she snagged a fool with connections to a duke and duchess?

"Well, if you're so easily trapped, then you deserve your fate."

Quincy fisted his palms at his brother's unfeeling remark. It was all logic and cool headedness with William. He had no heart. He had no understating of passion and how it bewitched the mind. He had never known such an outbreak of ecstasy or its potentially ruinous effects.

Quincy seethed between clenched teeth. "I won't marry the wench." He would not let her steal his likeness *and* his life.

"Then leave," said his brother.

"What?"

"Leave this house, leave my ship, leave England. And never return."

For a second, Quincy's heart stopped pumping. A coldness came over him; the ice pierced him right to the bone. "You would banish me?"

"You banish yourself if you choose to disgrace Miss Turner and her teenage sister, making them pariahs. This isn't the sea, Quincy, and you're not a pirate anymore. You can't take what you want, consequences be damned."

William stalked from the bedroom without another word, without even a gesture of encouragement or support or compassion.

Quincy cursed his stonehearted brother, willing a tempestuous wench to one day storm his orderly life and wreck it to bits.

But his anger quickly shifted back to Holly, and the coldness returned, rooted itself deep in his heart.

CHAPTER 5

Holly ignored the stinging heat from the wood burning stove as she threw sketch after charcoal sketch into the snapping flames. She had to clear out her art studio, a converted potting shed at the rear of the cottage. In light of the scandal she'd caused, she had no choice but to sell the little house on the outskirts of London and move with her sister to France or Switzerland. Perhaps salacious gossip would not follow them to the Continent.

After burning a large pile of female nudes, she came across her drawings of *him*. Her heart throbbed and her fingers trembled as she gazed into his mesmerizing eyes, hooded under dark brows. She had sketched him from memory, and her memories of him had been dreamlike in nature. Soon she had realized her previous portraits had been rigid, anatomical studies. *His* painting had been her first truly inspired work.

A lump welled in her throat until she had the most unladylike urge to scream. She slipped his likeness into the fire, sheet after detailed sheet of his eyes, his lips, his muscular shoulders, his naked backside, until only one illustration remained.

For a moment, she considered keeping the last pictorial of him but quickly dismissed the fancy and tossed it into the consuming flames. She watched the charred paper curl and blacken and finally turn to ash, much like her life.

Holly heaved a deep breath. After years of seclusion, hoping for the day when she and her sister might return to the folds of the upper crust, she had ruined everything by chasing after Mr. Hawkins. She should have found another, more appropriate time to beseech his discretion, but she had feared so many things. What if he refused to ever see her again? What if he went straight from the ball to the gossip sheets and revealed her identity as Lord H?

Ironically, her identity as the erotic artist remained a secret. But now the whole world believed her the man's mistress.

She took another deep breath to calm her pounding pulse. A benevolent gentleman might do the honorable thing and ask for her hand in marriage, saving her reputation, but Mr. Hawkins had confessed he only pretended to be a gentleman. Besides, almost two days had passed since the shameful incident without a single word from him.

Holly had no hope.

Pushing aside her grief, she next found a melancholy rendering of her mother. She traced the outline of the woman's fine profile with her fingertips, her lips quivering with longing. How she missed her mother's encouraging voice and high spirits. Her sparkling, effervescent laughter and tight, comforting embraces.

It had pained the viscountess beyond measure, quitting society and all its privileges after the disgraceful death of their father. A few loyal friends, like Lady Brimsby, had written to the woman with news and other babble, but the estrangement from the glittering world she had known and loved had broken her heart. And like a songbird trapped in a cage, their mother's musical voice had turned mournful, then silent. Even the companionship of her daughters had not been enough to assuage her sorrow. She had simply withered away and died.

Holly set aside the drawing of her mother as a keepsake. Her soul swirled with both dark and bright memories, lost hopes, then renewed faith. The welter reached its zenith when she came across the last image in the pile.

Her lips pinched as she stared at the sophisticated portrait of her late father, David Turner, Viscount Cavendish, with his neatly trimmed beard and well manicured moustache. She had captured the kindness in his eyes and his love for pleasure in the old sketch. But the longer she studied the image, the more her fingers squeezed the paper until it creased and distorted his tender face.

"Stop, Papa! Stop this instance!"

Her father lifted his defeated head. "I cannot stop, Holly. Not until I've restored everything that I've lost."

"If you do not stop now we will all perish."

"Holly, trust me. I will make things right."

"No," she cried. "I do not trust you anymore, Papa."

The viscount had adored his family—but not as much as he'd adored gambling. While there was nothing uncommon about a wealthy lord wagering at the card table, Holly's father had taken the pastime to an extreme, losing the family fortune. He had then committed an even greater transgression by taking his life and abandoning his wife and children in poverty.

She would never forgive her father for his reckless, selfish behavior. He had wrecked all their lives. And now, perhaps fittingly, Holly had soiled the already tainted Turner name, for her sin was now her sister's sin. Her misfortune, Emma's misfortune. And their lives were about to change in dramatic fashion. Again.

Holly threw the likeness of her father into the fire and closed the iron door with a thick wool rag. She then collected a sharp knife from the nearby table, prepared to slash every canvas in the studio.

She started.

In the doorframe, a shoulder against the wood, arms folded across his wide chest was Mr. Hawkins. He was dressed in riding attire, his wind-whipped locks loose around his sensual face, his smoldering eyes on her with great intent.

She resented her inescapable response to his presence, the shivers that rolled down her spine, the palpitations of her heart, and she gripped the knife even harder in her fist.

His gaze dropped to the blade. "Planning murder, Miss Turner?"

"Of a sort."

She walked over to the nearest canvas, removed the drape and stabbed the unnamed image. She twisted her wrist and sliced the canvas over and over again until the portrait was unrecognizable.

She then skirted toward another, unfinished painting. "What are you doing here, Mr. Hawkins?"

As she carved the second canvas, she sensed his movements at her backside and stiffened.

"I've come to tell you we're getting married."

Holly paused, her heart in her throat. Had she heard the rake right?

Slowly she turned around, the knife still in her quivering hand. "What?"

"I trust you will be sensible about the matter, Miss Turner."

Holly opened, then closed her lips. He had come to propose? "Now?"

"I beg your pardon?"

"You've come to propose *now*? Not yesterday? Not the night the scandal broke?"

He shrugged. "I wasn't in a rush to tie a noose around my neck."

Her grief, fear and humiliation, cramped inside her for almost two days, escaped her throat in a gasp or cry or croaking shriek, she wasn't sure. She dropped the knife and stared at him, incredulous.

"My brother-in-law, the duke, has procured a special license," he went on in the same flat vein. "We'll be married tomorrow."

"How could you do this?"

He glowered at her. "Do what?"

"Make me wait? I thought you had forsaken me? I thought I would have to leave England, uproot my sister."

"It was only fair under the devious circumstances."

"What devious circumstances?"

"You trapped me into marriage," he growled, his eyes alight. "If you suffered for it a few days, I'm delighted. *I* will have to suffer for it a lifetime."

He thought she had trapped him? On purpose? "I would *never* do such a hateful thing?"

"If you insist, Miss Turner."

"I do insist. I have integrity, Mr. Hawkins."

He gathered his stormy features and resumed his uniform tone. "Our wedding will be a simple affair. My sister will collect and escort you to the church. She will also host a private luncheon at her home in Mayfair."

"I did *not* trap you, Mr. Hawkins. If I wanted to snare a man, I would not have chosen a rake who only 'pretended' to be a gentleman. I would have picked a real gentleman, someone I was sure would propose."

He eyed her, dubious. "You've put a lot of thought into snaring a hapless man, haven't you?"

"Ugh!"

"Are you being unreasonable, Miss Turner? Are you refusing to marry me?"

"No!" With less heat in her voice, she said, "I am most sensible about the matter. I just don't want you to think so poorly of me . . . if I'm to be your wife."

"You are to be my wife." His voice dropped an octave. "Do not think otherwise."

She shivered at the unbending steel in his voice. "But why — ?"

"I would do anything for my sister."

As would Holly. If only her reputation had been ruined, she would carry her shame alone and move across the channel to start a new life. She would flout convention and refuse the man's offer of marriage. But she had her sister to protect. If there was an honorable way to restore her name, and thus her innocent sibling's, Holly would take it—however unfair to Mr. Hawkins.

"I understand," she said. "Your sister is most gracious, considering the embarrassment I caused her with my painting."

"She doesn't know you are Lord H."

Holly balked. The man had promised to guard her secret identity from society, but she had assumed he'd at least tell his sister. Otherwise . . .

"Why does your sister believe we're marrying in such haste?"

"She thinks I've seduced you, of course."

"But you haven't seduce me, Mr. Hawkins."

He had bewitched her, aye. Tormented her dreams. But seduction? The one time he'd truly tempted her with his seductive ways was on the night they'd first met at the gaming hell. Holly would never forget their short time together, the way he had looked at her with such longing, the way he had teased her with his playful charm.

She shuddered at the memory. How would it feel to be seduced by him again? To be seduced by her husband? Her blood warmed at the inviting thought. She imagined a future time when he didn't shoot daggers at her with his eyes, but caressed her with passionate want. And she found her flesh tingling with anticipation and hope.

Bemused, she asked, "Why would you let your sister think such a thing?"

"She expects it of me," he returned with indifference. "And better she thinks ill of me than my wife. She'll forgive me in time. She always does."

Holly's chest cramped again. He would carry the brunt of her disgrace, even at the loss of his sister's good opinion of him? She realized then how little she knew about her future spouse. He was more gallant than she'd imagined.

"But there is one caveat I insist upon, Miss Turner. You are not to carry on as Lord H, is that clear?"

She nodded. In truth, she was relieved to retire the pseudonym. It had preserved her and her sister in times of want, but it had also carried a dangerous risk of discovery and persecution.

For the first time in her adult life, Holly realized she was safe. From poverty. From exile. From arrest. Her legs wavered as the burden lifted from her shoulders, and she grabbed an easel for support.

Mr. Hawkins crouched and retrieved the knife from the floor. Blade in hand, he handed her the handle. "I'll leave you to finish what you've started. Good day, Miss Turner."

She took the knife from him and watched his towering figure depart. As soon as he'd saddled his horse and galloped away, she dropped to the ground and released her tears.

CHAPTER 6

Quincy stood beside the tall window, nursing his fourth glass of wine. He surveyed the small wedding party of nine, making merry in his sister's dining parlor. He had hoped the wine would take effect and dull his senses, but he was too accustomed to the drink. He needed opium to stifle the growing ache in his gut.

Edmund slapped him on the shoulder. "Congratulations, pup."

Quincy glowered at his disagreeable brother and bit out, "Thank you." He wasn't in a celebratory mood, and Edmund knew it. Still, his abrasive kin insisted on the felicitous pretense.

"She's a fine lass," said Edmund. "Amy's taken a shining to her."

Quincy eyed his wife, laughing with Lady Amy, the woman of Edmund's heart. As if sensing Quincy's stare, Miss T—Mrs. Hawkins looked away from Lady Amy and met his gaze, her leaf green eyes shining, then quickly lowered her reddish lashes, uncertain, perhaps even insecure. Her strawberry-flaxen locks were twisted and pinned in whimsy, tiny white flowers nestled amid the curls, while her dress, a sunset rose with lace trimmings, made her lips glow all the more pink.

She was fetching, he mused. And he felt an involuntary spasm in his chest. He had not expected to admire his wife on their wedding day — on the day she had taken away his freedom.

Quincy returned his attention to the window, downing the last of the wine, signaling the footman for another glass. "Lady Amy isn't privy to my wife's true character. She might not take such a shining to her then."

"Amy has sharp instincts. If she likes Holly, then she's a fine lass. Or are you suggesting Amy's 'true character' is also based on her sordid past?"

At the unmistakable growl in his brother's voice, Quincy raised a hand in peace. Lady Amy was the daughter of the Duke and Duchess of Estabrooke. She was currently married to the Marquis of Gravenhurst, their betrothal arranged at her birth. She had tried to break the betrothal contract to be with Edmund, but fate had not been kind to the star-crossed lovers. She had wed the marquis, as destined, though her husband was a monster. If not for Edmund, the marquis would have murdered Amy on their wedding night. The fiend had disappeared, and despite Edmund's best efforts to locate the marquis and charge him with Amy's attempted murder, Gravenhurst remained at liberty.

Quincy remembered the moment he had stood beside Edmund outside the Estabrooke townhouse, watching the wedding party toss rose petals at the newlyweds. The despair etched across his brother's face had pierced his own heart. The couple seemed doomed to be apart. But another twist of fate had rekindled their hope. It was discovered the marquis had married a barmaid long ago in a drunken stupor, making his marriage to Lady Amy unlawful. With evidence of bigamy in hand, the Consistory Courts in the Doctors' Commons had no choice but to grant Amy an annulment, even with Gravenhurst in hiding. The legal process might take several more months, but soon, one day, the couple would be married.

"No," said Quincy, accepting a fifth glass of wine from the footman. "I don't believe Lady Amy's true character is based on her sordid past. I admire her, you know that."

Edmund humphed in approval. "Then there's no reason to suspect you won't be happy with your wife. Her past as Lord H doesn't mean she isn't a fine woman."

After another hardy thump on the shoulder, Edmund moved off, and William took his place.

"You did the right thing, Quincy."

Quincy frowned. "I'm pleased you approve, old man."

His brother ignored the caustic remark. "We sail at first light. Will that be a problem?"

"Why should it?" he queried, taking another gulp of wine.

"It's your wedding night. Your wife might not appreciate your hasty departure and subsequent long absence."

"Do not trouble yourself with my *wife*. I'll be aboard the *Nemesis* at dawn."

William remained silent for what seemed an uncomfortable stretch of time, and Quincy was about to tell his older brother to bugger off, when he offered:

"I hope you and Holly will be happy together."

As William walked away, Quincy glared after him, unconvinced the man's good wishes were genuine.

The bloody parade of salutations continued with his brother-in-law, Damian, the Duke of Wembury, who approached him, glass in hand. "A toast."

"To what?"

Damian chuckled. "Your wife, of course."

Quincy maintained his frown as he clinked glasses with Damian. He had formed a friendship with the reformed "Duke of Rogues." Damian had saved his life many years ago in a pub brawl. And even after he had married Mirabelle, Quincy had accepted the man as kin. His three older brothers had yet to fully welcome the duke into the family. Or admit that he truly loved their sister with unbound passion. But Quincy hadn't the blind spot his brothers possessed when it came to romantic love. Whenever one of his sibling's had fallen under cupid's spell, Quincy had been the first to see it.

His ribs suddenly throbbed as his heart pounded ever harder and he dropped further into inescapable doldrums. Something inexplicable pressed on him, and he hadn't the word for the disturbing sensation.

"Quincy, a word, please."

He hardened at the tart sound of his sister's voice. With a sigh, he turned and confronted the duchess, her golden brows pinched together, her umber eyes alight. According to his eldest brothers, Mirabelle was the spitting image of their mother, while the rest of them resembled their father.

Quincy had no portrait of his mother, but he'd often looked at Mirabelle and imagined the woman's likeness. She had died in childbirth to him. His arrival into the world had caused his family much sorrow. His father had grieved for his wife until the end of his years. James and William, nineteen and seventeen at the time of her death, had reared the rest of them, ages newborn to four, until they'd grown of age.

Quincy had unsettled all their lives with his birth. At times, he even suspected his kin resented him for it. How could they not?

He peered more deeply into his sister's eyes. She, too, had almost died while giving birth to her second child, a son. At the gruesome memory, talons of fear gripped his heart. The crisis had turned his world on its ear. Ever since her near death two years ago, Quincy had chased the dragon to escape his own hellish guilt, for he couldn't shake the feeling that he had killed his mother — and wrecked all his siblings lives.

Mirabelle softened her furrowed brow. "Are you all right, Quincy?"

"Aye." He glanced away. "You'd like a word?"

"I hope to see the last of your romps and mischief," she said with less edge in her voice. "I trust you will look after Holly and her sister, as is proper."

"I appreciate your faith in me, Belle."

Damian tipped his glass. "I think I'll sample the

cake."

As soon as her husband strutted off, Mirabelle sighed. "I didn't mean to suggest you were irresponsible."

He quirked a brow.

"All right, I did. But I also know you're a good man, Quincy. I hope you will settle happily in your new position as husband."

If one more person wished him happiness in marriage, Quincy would crush the glass in his hand. "Thank you, Belle."

She sighed again and joined her husband at the dessert table. For a blessed moment, Quincy had peace. But it wasn't long before his ears burned again.

"I must congratulate you, Quincy."

His sister-in-law, Sophia, walked over to him, smiling and removing her gloves. Born and raised on the island of Jamaica, she was a strong, spirited woman who matched his eldest brother, James, in every way. The couple had married sixteen months ago, and it was something of a sensation that the most forbidding of all his siblings had actually wed — and was content.

"If James were here, I'm sure he would do the honors," she said.

Captain James Hawkins was currently aboard the *Bonny Meg*, named after their mother, Megan. The mighty schooner had once plundered the high seas under the rule of the infamous pirate, Black Hawk. But like the rest of his kin, James had retired his fearsome epithet and now sailed the *Bonny Meg* as a merchant vessel.

"If James were here, he'd break my legs," quipped Quincy, "and you know it."

Her exotic brown eyes burnished with laughter. She had an infernal sense of humor, much like her husband.

"Then perhaps it's a good thing you posed nude *and* seduced an innocent lass while he was at sea."

"A boon, indeed," he grumbled.

The woman laughed, a throaty sound. "I'm not so bothered by your winsome ways. I'm a pirate's daughter, remember? I've done worse."

She winked and skirted off, and Quincy was glad to know at least one member of his family wasn't going to box his ears over his "winsome ways."

Once more, Quincy glanced at his wife, now ensconced with her teenage sister in a tête-à-tête. Their wedding had been simple. The duke and duchess had escorted the bride to the church. Edmund had served as groom's man, young Emma as bride's maid. The ceremony had been somber, thus respectable. A wedding announcement would appear in tomorrow's broadsheet, saving everyone's reputation.

Quincy had done his duty. And in so doing, he had given away his freedom, his future . . .

His heart spasmed again, and he finally recognized the nameless sentiment that afflicted his soul: loss. He had lost the opportunity to find love. Unlike the rest of his siblings, he would never have the chance to choose his spouse — and be happy.

He had given far too much to his new bride. And he vowed right then he would give her nothing more. Ever.

CHAPTER 7

Holly sat beside her sister in the carriage, rattling along the pebbled road. From under her lowered lashes, she peeked at her strapping husband, sitting in the opposite squab. He gazed out the window, impervious. He hadn't said a word during their journey to her cottage. Emma had prattled about the day, how pretty everyone had looked, how delicious the food, but even she had grown reticent. And now the small party of three travelled in total silence.

Holly wasn't sure what to make of the lull. Was her husband fatigued? Angry? Anxious about their wedding night?

Her fists scrunched, Holly unfurled her stiff fingers and released a tense breath. She was certainly nervous about the wedding night. She had never been with a man. And to be with *this* man? She had already seen him naked—every part of him—and her heart sounded like heavy bell tolls at the intimate thought of being with him . . . being one with him.

She removed her gloves, her fingers moist beneath the fabric. Her lungs cramped and she seemed starved for air, panting. She tried to hide her unraveling disposition, but her sister sensed her distress and rubbed her arm.

"Are you well, Holly?"

"I'm fine," she whispered, her voice strained.

Her husband turned toward her at the remark, his eyes inscrutable under the growing darkness. But she felt his sharp focus on her. He remained quiet, though, and soon returned his attention to the bucolic landscape.

The drive from London had taken over an hour, and it was dusk by the time they reached the little house in the country.

Quincy stepped out of the vehicle first and extended his hand, supporting the ladies as they descended the carriage.

The maid and gardener, a married, childless pair, emerged from the house and greeted the newlyweds. The young farm hand, Robert, was also there and quickly assisted the driver with the luggage.

Holly glanced at her husband. "Are you hungry? I had a light supper prepared for our return."

"No," he said softly. "It's been a long journey. I'd rather stretch my legs in the garden."

He offered her a curt bow before disappearing between the neatly trimmed hedges and rose bushes.

She tensed at his abrupt departure. Why hadn't he offered her guidance? A simple hint as to what she should do next?

After an indecisive moment, Holly entered the house. She instructed the maid to put away supper, then directed her husband's belongings to her bedroom. Emma and Robert exchanged blushing glances. The maid and gardener exchanged knowing ones.

Holly's own cheeks warmed as she hurried up the crooked stairs to her chamber, unwilling to endure their ribbing humor. She slipped inside her room, and after the baggage had been delivered, closed the door, releasing another buried breath.

The duchess had offered her and Quincy quarters for the night, but her husband had declined the invitation, perhaps uncomfortable at the thought of spending his wedding night under his sister's roof. He could not return with her to his bachelor residence in St. James's. It was wholly improper. And so they'd travelled back to her cottage, a consequence of their madcap marriage. There had been no time to prepare new living arrangements in the city, a wedding tour or even a trousseau. In the coming weeks, there was much to plan and organize.

But first, the wedding night.

The bedroom had been carefully readied: fresh linens, a warm fire, burning lamps. Holly inhaled the soothing fragrance of jasmine, the yellow flowers cut fresh from the garden and sitting in a vase on the window sill.

Right, she thought. It's time.

Gathering her nerves, she sidestepped the luggage and entered the adjoining bathing room. A small tin tub had been filled with water, now lukewarm, but Holly was too frazzled to care about the temperature. She divested her garments and quickly washed. She then slipped into a white night rail and covered herself with a wrapper. She loosed her hair, removed the tiny flowers and combed the curls. Finally, she sat on the edge of the bed. And waited. And waited.

After several more fruitless minutes, she approached the window and gazed into the dark garden, illuminated by soft moonlight. It was hard to tell between the trees and shrubs if a figure stood amidst the bramble. As she scouted the terrain, her eyes soon spotted a man's tall build. He remained fixed beside the garden gate, his hands at his backside, wanting to escape?

Holly settled on the window sill next to the vase and watched him. Her husband. She had a sacred place in his life now, that of wife. And he equally shared a sacred place in hers, that of husband. But she had done him great harm, forcing him into wedlock. And she vowed to be a good wife, a pleasing wife. She would make amends to him — somehow.

His shadow shifted and he turned toward the house, his eyes lifting to her. Her breath trapped in her throat as he studied her with unwavering intent. At last he ambled across the lawn toward the house.

Holly quickly returned to the bedside, her heart booming like canon blasts. She had already kissed him once, a fiery explosion of feeling. She wanted to taste him again. To touch him. And as she heard his heavy steps ascend the creaking stairs, she gasped for air.

He stopped at the door. She noticed his shoes under the crack. After a brief pause, he rapped on the wood.

"Come in," she all but croaked.

He opened the barrier. His sensual blue eyes

settled on her as his robust frame filled the small space. He had loosened his cravat and waistcoat, his cuff links, too. His informal attire suggested more was to be removed, and she pinched the fabric of her wrapper in anticipation.

He was beautiful, she thought. And she had a deep yearning to explore his beauty. She wondered if he found her as attractive. Would he kiss her with the same spirited hunger as he had on the night of the ball? Or had their unexpected marriage hardened his desire for her? She hoped not. They were virtual strangers. But they shared a mutual heat. From the night they'd first met at the gaming hell that fire had burned between them. It wasn't the strongest foundation to build a marriage upon, for a fire, if unattended, could burn out. But it was a foundation.

A beginning.

He reached for his luggage. "I've come to collect my belongings."

Her heart dropped. "I-I don't understand."

"I'll be leaving in a few hours, and I don't want to disturb you at dawn. The maid tells me there's a third bedroom around the corner. I will take that chamber."

Her mother's old room. But why? "Where are you going in the morning?"

"To sea."

She gaped, stunned. "You are a sailor?"

"I am."

She couldn't believe her ears. He *was* a sailor. Her clandestine source had been right about his identity. But why had Quincy withheld the truth from her until now?

"But . . . I . . ." She fumbled, confused. "How long will you be away?"

"Three months, at least."

"I see." She twined her fingers. "Are you an officer?"

"A privateer. I serve alongside my brother, William, in the Royal Navy's African Squadron. I'm the ship's surgeon."

"A doctor?"

He shook his head. "I've no formal training. I studied under the previous surgeon."

Holly sensed a tightness in her throat. He would be absent much of the time. "What will become of Emma and I? Where will we live?"

In the rickety cottage? On the fringe of society?

"Choose whatever house you'd like in Town," he said, indifferent. "I have a few furloughs each year and spend little time on land, so I'm not particular about our abode. I'm sure my sister will help you find an appropriate dwelling. She's rather fond of you, I'm told."

Of course the duchess was fond of her, compassionate toward her, even commiserating. The woman believed her an innocent damsel seduce by her rakish brother.

Holly winced at the grisly falsehood.

Quincy headed toward the door.

"Wait!"

He stilled. "What is it?"

She lifted from the bedside, her legs shaking. "What about tonight? Our wedding night?"

He turned toward her again, his eyes charged with fierce resistance. "Do not assume our marriage is real, *wife*. It is in name alone. What you took of my body and put in that infernal painting is all you will *ever* take of me."

He stalked from the room, leaving the door ajar.

Holly blanched. She dropped backward, plopping onto the bed. She would *never* be with her husband? She would never run her fingers across his rolling muscles or feel the heat of his flesh beneath her hands? She would never taste his sensuous lips again or hear his seductive voice in her ear, arousing her senses? She would never know the intimate feel of him inside her? Or have children? Ever?

Her heart ballooned. Her lungs expanded like storm clouds. To be leg shackled in matrimony without any of the sensual benefits was unrighteous. And Holly wouldn't stand for it. Her husband desired her, she knew it. He'd revealed a fervent passion for her on the eve he'd ravaged her with his covetous lips. And she *would* have him again. All of him. Even if she had to seduce the stubborn rake.

CHAPTER 8

Quincy leaned against the starboard rail, watching the *Nemesis* navigate through the Thames. As the schooner neared port, the noise, bustle and stench of sewage bombarded his senses, and he slowly adjusted to the turbulence of city life.

His disorderly thoughts drifted with the current toward the bright lights of Town, and he wondered about his wife. During a sea voyage, he usually refrained from opium. His mind tended to clear amid the waves and stars, and he needn't the drug's amnesic effect. But Holly had followed him aboard ship, the wench. He had sensed her presence throughout the journey, heard her silky voice, tasted her wanton lips. And he had searched for respite in opium paste. Instead, he had found only more hellish suffering. She had breached the foggy barrier in his mind and had teased him in his dreams with her promises of a sensual wedding night.

After three celibate months at sea, Quincy ached for a woman, for the warmth of a supple body in his arms and the taste of sweetly perfumed skin. He remembered his wife's wild strawberry tresses and slender figure under a slim white wrapper. His blood heated and his muscles hardened as he heard her inviting voice calling him to bed.

But he would not bed her.

Ever.

His lust for her would burn out in time. Then, he would be free of her. He would always provide her protection from gossip and the security of a house. But he would never offer her a part of himself. She had his money, his name. And no more. She had already stolen too much from him . . . like a bloody pirate.

A figure approached Quincy in the dusky light. He recognized his brother's build. William had been unusually thoughtful throughout the voyage. On several occasions, Quincy had found him reflective, staring out at sea, instead of patrolling the decks or scouring the waters with his spyglass or journaling in his captain's log. He wondered what had captivated his brother's mind.

William settled beside him. "We're third in the queue. It should be another hour or so before we dock."

Quincy had reconciled with his brother, not in words, but the men had grown comfortable eating together at the same table in the mess hall or sharing sea shanties with the crew.

In truth, there was no cause to resent his sibling for his unfortunate marriage. That honor belonged to Holly. *She* had painted him without his permission and released the work into society. *She* had recklessly followed him to his carriage in public view. *She*, and she alone, had trapped him in wedlock, intentionally or not.

"Care for a pint after we dock?" asked Quincy, hoping to avoid his wife for as long as possible.

"I have to prepare my final report. I meet with the Admiralty in the morning."

Quincy sensed something was amiss in his brother's stiff voice. "Is there trouble with the Admiralty?"

Their tour had been routine. The only real threats had been the merciless heat and heavy rains off Africa's west coast. Regrettably, most British slavers sailed with foreign flags and papers, preventing the *Nemesis* from legally apprehending the ships. But a few brazen captains still sailed under the Union Jack, and it was those brash ships the *Nemesis* hunted and battled.

"No, no trouble," returned William.

It was still there in his voice, that reflective, almost absentminded tone. What had distracted the otherwise highly focused captain?

Quincy thought of asking him outright. He never withheld his opinions or queries and that penchant sometimes—always—got him into trouble. But he sensed it wasn't the right moment to invade his brother's pensiveness.

"I suppose I should go home then." Quincy heaved a deep breath. He would rather rove the high seas until he'd strangled every carnal impulse he had for his wife. "I wonder where I live?"

A rare chuckle from William. "Head back to St. James's. I'm sure Eddie knows your new address. And send word to Belle that we're safe. You know how she worries while we're at sea."

"Aye, Captain."

After more than an hour, the *Nemesis* finally docked in the Thames. A rugged Quincy with his bushy beard and tousled curls disembarked the ship. Slinging his pack of possessions over his shoulder, he wended through the blusterous throng, heading for his old bachelor abode.

By the time he reached the townhouse, it was dark. The butler greeted him at the door and informed him Edmund was not at home.

"Where is he?"

"With Her Grace, the Duchess of Wembury."

At such a late hour? An unbidden memory invaded his mind—his sister's ashen face, her hopeless sobs of grief. He shut his eyes against the tortuous images, his chest tightening. He had yet to harden his soul against the nightmarish visions. And he wondered . . . he wondered if they would haunt him forever.

"What's happened, Benson? Is she unwell?"

"Her Grace is in excellent health, sir."

Quincy released the breath trapped in his throat.

"She is hosting the engagement ball for Mr. Hawkins and Lady Amy."

"The annulment between Lady Amy and Gravenhurst is final?"

"Indeed, sir."

"Ha! That's wonderful news. I have to change."

Quincy dashed into the house and pounded the stairs.

"Your belongings are not here, sir."

He stilled. Of course not. Damn! "Where are

they?"

"Mrs. Hawkins had them moved to your new residence in Grosvenor Square."

"That's on the other side of Mayfair."

"Indeed, sir."

There wasn't time to travel to Grosvenor Square, change his attire and shave. He'd miss the ball!

Quincy looked up the stairs. "I'll have to burrow Eddie's togs. Send up hot water, Benson. I stink like the Thames. And fetch me a runner!"

In less than an hour, Quincy had shaved his whiskers, bathed and donned his brother's fancy duds. He'd also penned a note about the ball and paid a runner a full pound to deliver the message to William in all haste aboard the *Nemesis*.

Quincy then took to the congested roads by horseback, sidestepping the blockade of carriages, and reaching his sister's swanky townhouse just before eleven in the evening.

The crush indoors was unmaneuverable, worse than the choked Thames. Flowers filled the ballroom, hanging in swags from windows, pouring from urns on pedestals, and reaching toward ceilings in tall ceramic vases. Brilliant candlelight burned the eyes. And melted wax filled the lungs with its scorching thickness.

After several minutes, Quincy spotted the engaged couple performing a waltz. Without misgiving, he crossed the floor, weaving between the other spinning dancers, and elbowed his way between the twosome.

"Quincy!" Amy threw her arms around his neck, and he crushed her in a tight hold, twirling her in the air. She gasped when he set her back on her feet. "I'm so glad you've returned in time to be Edmund's groom's man."

"When is the wedding?"

"In a month's time."

"In the heat of summer? You won't wait until the spring?"

"I've waited almost a *year* to marry your brother. I'll not wait another, no matter how unfashionable."

He grinned. "I couldn't be happier for you, Amy." He next turned toward his brother and extended his hand. "Congratulations, Eddie."

Edmund pushed aside the offered hand and embraced him. "Thank you."

Quincy laughed. His surly brother wasn't the sort to express affection. The man's inspiring fiancée had spurred the uncharacteristic sentiment, Quincy was sure.

"I sent word to William aboard the *Nemesis*. He should be here soon."

"I'm glad to hear it," said Edmund. "Welcome home, Quincy. And look out. James is heading straight for you."

Edmund then swooped his intended bride away.

Quincy groaned. He turned and witnessed his eldest brother cutting a line through the dance floor, intimidated couples whisking out of his path. The generational gap between him and James, almost forty-two years of antiquity, placed them in the more contentious positions of father and son, rather than siblings. Quincy was closer with Edmund in more ways than age, though. They had both endured "the rules" of their controlling older brother.

"Hullo, James."

James was taller than him by two scant inches but brandished the most formidable features, his long black hair tied in a queue, his blue eyes always hinting of violence. He of all his brethren had endured the most difficult transition from pirate to gentleman. His gruff ways and inhospitable manner had made him an outcast, earning him the reputation of "barbarian" in high society — until he'd "killed" the pirate Black Hawk.

James had staged his own death to protect their pasts and secure their futures, and he'd become the nation's hero for ridding the waves of the infamous rogue. There was irony there, somewhere, thought Quincy, that to live, one first had to die.

Quincy wondered if his own death was looming, his brother's gaze inscrutable.

"I understand you're married," said James.

Quincy waited for the rest of the sentence, the inevitable reproach, the thrashing, and when all failed to follow, he frowned. "And?"

His expression stony, James reached out his hand. "And congratulations."

In a wary move, Quincy returned the handshake. "Thank you."

"I admire your wife. She's a spirited lass."

And with that unexpected compliment, James sauntered off, leaving Quincy bewildered in the middle of the dance floor. Where was the tirade? The broken legs?

He stared after his brother, who joined his wife near an alcove beside the musicians stand. Sophia lifted a glass and smiled at Quincy. He returned the salutation, still stumped.

Quincy hadn't a moment more to mull over the inexplicable exchange with his brother when his sassy sister scooped him in her arms and whirled him across the dance floor.

"You've returned," she said with a mumpish frown. "Good. I've a bone to pick with you."

As he waltzed with her, his ill humor darkened. First, he had to contend with his brother's queer behavior. And now Mirabelle was making an unjustified fuss. He had been at sea for three bloody months! How could he have made a blunder and grieved her?

"What bone?" he demanded.

"Why didn't you tell me Holly was Lord H?"

Quincy missed a step. "How did you find out?"

"She told me, of course."

"The devil she did!"

What was the wench doing, confessing her notorious identity as the erotic artist? To his sister, no less?

Quincy scanned the ballroom, peering over winding couples, searching for his wayward wife. Soon he spotted her across the room, radiant in a bronze satin gown, her strawberry locks appearing more golden under the burnished candlelight. He also noticed she was surrounded by mooning, winking, lustful men.

Quincy saw red.

CHAPTER 9

Holly had sensed her husband's presence the moment he'd entered the ballroom; the air had changed somehow, the nattering men around her had dissolved like ghosts into obscurity. She searched the crowd and as soon as she spotted him, her heart stomped with the unbridled passion of a race horse eager to take to the tracks—and win.

He had bronzed in the African sun, she mused. His muscles had swelled. His wavy black hair had grown unfashionably long, but he'd smoothed the tresses behind his ears, soft curls stroking his chiseled jaw line.

She had missed him. He had been her husband for a single day before he'd gone to sea. And yet she had missed him. Or perhaps she had missed the desire to know him better. He had left her wanting, yearning for more than a marriage of convenience.

Holly observed his every movement, waiting for the moment he'd look in her direction. He had greeted his brothers and was dancing with his sister at present, his features a scowl. Whatever their conversation, it wasn't a pleasant reunion. Suddenly he stumbled, then his head snapped up and he scoured the ballroom.

When his smoldering eyes lighted on her, a shot of pure pleasure ripped down her spine. He stalked away from the duchess, leaving her on the dance floor with her arms akimbo, and headed straight for Holly.

Her skin sprouted gooseflesh, her lungs craved more air. The room grew hot, sweltering hot. The licentious men around her disbanded in haste. And then he was there. Her husband. Towering above her. Fire in his eyes.

"Welcome home, Quincy."

He hardened. It was the first time she had used his Christian name, and the implied intimacy had obviously unsettled him.

She smiled and lifted her gloved hand. "Shall we dance?"

Not only had her husband abandoned her on their wedding night with the unexpected declaration that they would never have a real marriage, but he'd also informed her he was a privateer, spending most of the year at sea chasing slavers.

The first revelation had struck her with dismay and eventually a hard-headed determination to improve her circumstances and become a *real* wife. The second revelation, however, had jarred her at a later date.

It had taken her a long while to accept the harsh possibility that one day her husband might not return from the sea, that a brutal storm or fierce clash with a slaver might take him away from her forever.

She shivered at the grim thought. But she needn't

fret about his wellbeing tonight. He had returned and in robust health. She could hold him in her arms and dance with him, not worry about his next tour of duty or even the next day.

After a brief hesitation, Quincy grasped her fingers and guided her toward the dance floor. She shuddered at the rough tenderness in his hold, and when he curled an arm around her waist and swept her across the room, she sighed with delight.

"How was your voyage?" she wondered in a warm manner, hiding the quiver in her heart. She really didn't want to hear about any near death escapes.

"Unremarkable."

"And William?"

"Alive."

His succinct answers, lacking any dangerous details, put her heart at ease and allowed her to focus on his sharp gaze instead, piercing her like arrowheads. She maintained his unwavering stare, wading in the dark blue pools of his eyes, relishing the passionate closeness.

"I purchased a house on Park Street," she announced in the same agreeable vein. "There is room for my sister, an art studio for myself and a separate bedroom for you." Though she'd every intention of changing that last unpleasant fact, right quick.

"You will *not* return to work as Lord H."

"I am capable of more than nudes, I assure you. I intend to paint for my own pleasure, any number of subjects. And I will not sell my work, nor expose it to public view. I must have a hobby."

Still he glowered. "Why did you reveal you identity as Lord H to Belle?"

Ah, the thorn in his side. In the three months since his departure, Holly had made earnest efforts to befriend her in-laws and had found their sincere welcome of her the most wonderful gift. But she'd been unable to accept their generosity on false pretenses. How could she build camaraderie with her new family without first being truthful about her past?

And so she'd confessed her identity as Lord H and the real reason behind her hasty marriage to their youngest brother, that he had not seduced her or acted in a dishonorable manner.

Holly had dreaded making the admission. She had finally found a secure situation in life, and she would risk it by revealing a scandalous secret? But her brother-in-law, Edmund, already privy to her former identity as Lord H, had welcomed her into the fold. Perhaps the others would as well? she'd reasoned.

Whatever the outcome, Holly would not allow the rest of the family to believe Quincy a blackguard. In the end, to her boundless relief, the Hawkins's had accepted her in spite of her sordid past.

"I revealed my former identity to your entire family," she corrected.

His features tightened. "Why?"

"To take the stain off your character, of course."

"Bully to that! Belle is still furious with me."

"She's furious with you because you allowed her to believe you were a dishonorable rake."

"Well, haven't you done me a world of good? She

now thinks I'm a liar instead of a dishonorable rake."

Holly flushed.

"I warned you to leave the matter alone, *wife*."

If he thought to reproach her for her defiance by playing the part of the dominant husband, he would first have to *be* her husband.

"I am a wife in name only, remember? And I will not always honor your wishes, *husband*."

The veins in his neck throbbed. "Is that so?"

"It is, indeed." And then she pressed her breasts against his hard chest, touched his ear with her lips and whispered, "But if you ever care to be a real husband, do let me know."

And with that invitation, she sashayed off the dance floor.

Quincy remained rooted to the dance floor. As resplendent couples twirled around him, the blood in his veins pounded with such ferocious intensity, he thought his head would burst from the pressure.

Had the audacious wench just disobeyed him *and* invited him to bed?

His fingers ticked, his cock stirred. He was going to cause a spectacle and ruin his brother's engagement ball.

In swift strides, Quincy stormed from the ballroom. He burst through the terrace doors and prowled the flagstone courtyard, searching for something to crush with his hands. When he discovered a bench, he slammed his fists into the seat, splintering the wood. He thought of turning the bench over and ramming it into the ground, when mordant laughter captured his senses.

"Piss off, James!"

His brother crossed the terrace with a knowing grin. "I once fractured my knuckles after a fight with Sophia, shoved my fist right into a wall."

"Is that why you're being such a charming ass? You know I'm in hell?"

"Aye."

Quincy clenched his palms, aching for a fight, but his sadistic brother wasn't going to give him one, relishing instead in his torment.

"I can't live with her, James."

He shrugged. "You spend most of the year at sea."

"I'll stay in a hotel when I'm on land."

"And spread rumor of an abandoned bride? You can't avoid her, Quincy. She's your wife."

And with another ruthless smirk, James sauntered back inside the ballroom, his last words hanging over Quincy like a noose.

She's your wife.

His innards twisted with want. Aye, she was his wife. And she was intent on her blasted wedding night. It wasn't enough he had saved her reputation? He had to surrender his body, too? Why? What did she want? Children?

Well, she could take a damn lover and have her infernal wedding night. He'd claim any of her offspring as his own. There were already hordes of men salivating over her now that she was wed, plenty of candidates to choose from.

A maiden was dangerous territory, always leading to wedlock—he knew firsthand—but a married woman was the perfect mistress, offering an affair without the risk of a nuptial entanglement.

As soon as the vision of another man grinding over his wife flashed through his mind, though, a murderous impulse streamed through his blood.

"You must be so tired after your long voyage."

Her gentle voice came over him like a hammer. He trembled with fury. And more. He trembled with unfathomable lust. He'd never wanted to bed a woman with such intensity in all his life. He doubted another wench would satisfy him—and that worried him.

Immensely.

Quincy girded his muscles as he turned toward the terrace doors and found his wife in angelic amity, the ballroom lights illuminating her shapely silhouette.

She had been spending his money carte blanche, he thought, nettled. She looked damned rich in her shimmering satin gown and bejeweled headpiece— and bloody beautiful, too. Her low cut bodice cupped her firm breasts, elongated her slender neck and framed her heart-shaped lips. He dragged in mouthfuls of air as his blood simmered with achingly familiar hunger.

"Shall we retire?" She stepped forward, her hips swinging. Her eyes narrowed on him with such intent, he shuddered. "I'll have the staff prepare your room. A light supper, too."

He imagined her in his bed, screaming his name as she orgasmed, drawing him deeper into her womb, and he shuddered again.

"No."

"All right, if you're not hungry."

"Oh, I'm hungry," he rasped, his erection pressing against his trousers. "I'll be at Madam Barovski's for the rest of the night."

He headed through the garden, pounding the grass.

"I'm afraid you're banned from Madam Barovski's establishment."

He stilled. "What?"

"She wants nothing more to do with you, not since your brother's visit to her gaming hell some months ago."

Slowly he turned toward her again. "Who told you this?"

"Your brother, Edmund."

Damn! Edmund had threatened the gaming mistress with ruination unless she confessed the identity of Lord H. Quincy would have to find another haunt to fulfill his needs.

Unbelievable. He'd yet another reason to throttle his wife.

And *why* was his wench-of-a-wife talking to Edmund about his haunts? Or conversing with James for that matter? Or Belle? And about such intimacies?

"I've already sent for the carriage," she said in a quaint, almost innocent manner. "You really should rest."

He gritted his teeth. She would not take what was left of him, he vowed. His body was his to give alone. And while he'd no experience resisting a luscious woman, he was determined to resist this one.

You can't avoid her. She's your wife.

She *was* his wife. And he would put her in her rightful place, make it clear to her there would be no wedding night between them.

Ever.

But how? He wasn't a brute. He usually charmed a woman into giving him what he wanted with a smile, a wink, a few craftily whispered words. He sure as hell couldn't charm his own wife, though.

Bullocks.

CHAPTER 10

As the carriage jounced through the gas illuminated streets, Holly clasped her hands in her lap—though she envisioned clasping them around her husband's throat. Imagine, returning from a dangerous three month voyage and outright confessing to a new, worried bride you were off to a den of sin to bed a whore!

It took every bit of her self-restraint to maintain an agreeable manner and amiable tone, and to keep from clobbering her husband with her shoe. The nerve. The bullheadedness. The *rake*. And she had defended his honor. What rubbish! She should have left the matter alone as he'd bidden her. Instead, she'd risked alienating her new family by confessing her scandalous past and ennobling her husband.

"Are you all right?"

Holly snapped her head away from the window and glared at the man. "What?"

"You're huffing," said Quincy. "Often."

Was she? "I'm fine. Tired, is all."

"Hmm." He crossed his arms over his chest and stretched out his long legs, bumping her shin. "It must be very tiring indeed, flirting with so many men?"

She shivered at his incidental touch. He had noticed the pack of roués, had he? She humphed. The men were an infernal nuisance, to use her husband's turn of phrase. She had once coveted such amorous attention, but since meeting her desirable husband, no other man had captured her interest.

Wait! Was Quincy jealous? She glanced at his furrowed brow and dark frown. A warmth settled in her belly at the delightful thought, and she decided to turn the frustrating situation into an advantageous one.

She smiled. "Yes, I shall have to acquire a little notebook to keep all their names straight in my mind."

The conversation ended there, followed by a tense silence. When the carriage rolled up to a flat faced townhouse with three rows of six paned windows and an elegant lintel above the front door, alight with sconces, Quincy exited the vehicle and climbed the front step, pounding on the door, leaving her unattended in the carriage.

Well, she'd ignited his jealousy. She only hoped she hadn't pushed him too far with the innuendo of other lovers. She had to keep the fire between *them* burning. If ever his disposition toward her changed, turned indifferent, their marriage would truly be in name only, having withered to ash.

She tottered from the vehicle before the driver whipped the horses and headed around the corner to the stables at the rear of the house.

The front door opened.

Quincy charged indoors, passing the aghast butler, and headed for the stairs.

"It's all right, Thompson," she assured the elderly servant as she stepped into the entrance hall. "Meet your new master, Mr. Hawkins." As Quincy mounted the stairs, she called after him, "Would you like me to give you a tour of the house?"

"No."

"You don't even know which bedroom is yours, though."

"I'll recognize my own bleedin' furniture."

He crossed the landing, disappearing from view, his heavy footfalls marching through the upstairs passageways.

Holly sighed. "He's tired," she reassured a frowning Thompson. "He has been at sea for months and needs rest. He's really rather charming otherwise."

The dubious butler nodded in silence and collected her shawl. "And Miss Turner?"

"Still at the ball. Captain and Mrs. Hawkins will escort her home."

Holly trusted Captain James Hawkins and his wife to chaperone her sister. One ominous glare from the imposing captain would squash any licentious intents toward Emma, so there was no reason to curtail the girl's fun with an early departure. Besides, Holly had hoped for time alone with her husband, a pleasant conversation over a late supper perhaps. Regrettably, her hopes had been dashed.

As she climbed the stairs, a stark bellow resounded through the house.

"Holly!"

She scowled. The *first* time her husband used her Christian name and it was in the tone of a disapproving parent. How ignoble. Was he mad? Had he *no* manners? His outrageous behavior was fodder for servant gossip. And what the devil was the matter now?

She rushed up the stairs, skirt in hands, and rounded the corner. She found the door to her art studio ajar — and smirked.

Holly smoothed her satin skirt before gracefully entering the room, ablaze with newly installed gas lamps. Her husband, searching for his own private chamber, had turned up the lights to discover her workspace and had obviously snooped around.

After closing the door, she asked in her most pleasant voice, "Yes?"

"What is *that* doing here?" he demanded, drape in hand. His features turned a crimson red as he pointed at the painting of himself, the sensual painting that'd caused so much trouble.

"It was found under your bed during the move from St. James's."

"*Why* is it still in one piece? I thought you had destroyed every infernal nude."

"I destroyed every nude in my studio at the cottage. This was not at my cottage. And since you had stored it under your bed . . ." She shrugged. "I thought you'd wanted to keep it."

"Are you mad? I wanted to burn the wretched thing, but our wedding and my tour at sea prevented me from torching it."

He headed for the door.

"Where are you going?" she cried.

"To fetch matches."

"No!" Holly dashed toward the door and barricaded it with her body. "You will not destroy that painting."

His body, heaving with fury, leaned over hers. "Move away from the door, wench."

"You can't burn it."

"I *own* it. I can do anything I damn well please with it."

"You also own this house. Will you burn it, too?"

"If it pleases me, aye."

She snorted. "A ridiculous reason. That painting is my greatest work. You will *not* destroy it."

"Your greatest work marks one of the worst moments in my life."

"Then don't come in here." She snatched the drape from his hand. "I didn't invite you into my private studio. I would like you to leave, please."

She hastened back to the artwork, veiling it to protect it from sunlight, dust and any paint splatter that might occur from future works.

Quincy glared at her from the door. "What about the servants? And your sister? I won't have anyone ogling that painting."

While Holly had hired new staff, she had also retained two of her former servants, the maid and gardener from the cottage. And she had already trained all the employees about the strict running of the household.

"The servants do not come into my studio, nor does Emma. Ever since I converted the potting shed at the cottage into an art studio, that has been the rule. No one will ever look at this painting, except me."

His breathing deepened, turned to rasps of air. "You?"

She confronted her husband again, his eyes glowing like embers. "Yes, me. If all I will ever have of you is what I took and put in this painting, then I will keep the painting and look at it whenever it pleases me."

Her declaration must have set off an explosive fire inside him, for his expression twisted, turning both tortuous and ravenous. Her own body flared with heat, and she longed for his primal touch, his sensuous kiss, but after a few strained moments, he swiveled his stone hard posture and left the room.

Holly sighed with a blend of disappointment and hope.

One day, she vowed.

One day she would have her husband.

CHAPTER 11

Quincy slammed the door of his bedchamber and prowled the room. He rent the cravat from his neck and stripped off his jacket and vest. That woman! That infernal woman! She would keep the wretched nude? Stare at it whenever it pleased her? Stare at *him* whenever it pleased her?

He kicked off his shoes, sending both into the wall. He'd torch that painting yet, he vowed. He wouldn't give her the pleasure of keeping it, of keeping *him*, like a sideshow bear trapped in a cage. She would not have any part of him, not even his likeness.

Pulling the shirt up over his head, he dropped it, too, to the floor. Was she staring at it right now? he wondered, then stopped in his tracks. His every muscle cramped at the thought of her penetrating eyes caressing the canvas, her elfin fingers grazing the fabric in sensual want.

As if he'd felt her arousing touch, he shuddered.

Burn it.

Definitely.

Quincy crouched beside the sea chest at the foot

of his bed and rummaged through the contents, searching for the satchel of opium capsules stored somewhere inside. He needed the drug's numbing effect, its blissful ability to blot out torments. He damn well didn't want to think about his wife wanting him. Or wanting other men.

He stilled as he remembered the lechers salivating over her during the engagement ball. And her "little notebook" of the men's names? Perhaps she'd already had an affair? He'd been gone three months and hadn't a deuced idea what she'd done — unsupervised — in all that time.

No, she wouldn't take a lover while he was at sea. If she became pregnant, it would be mighty obvious he wasn't the father. She would time her affairs with his furloughs, the wench. And if she was having an affair right now?

He fisted his palms. What if she was already pregnant? What if *that* was the real reason she was so intent upon their wedding night? To legitimate the babe?

He didn't care. He *shouldn't* care.

At last he found the satchel and grabbed a few capsules. He dropped his head back and downed the opium. The capsules became stuck at the back of his throat, but the sugar coating quickly melted and the drug slipped easily into his belly.

Quincy wiped his mouth and sighed, dropping the satchel back inside the chest. Soon, he thought. Soon the unfeeling darkness would come and he would rest.

He pushed away from the chest and peeled off his trousers before he dropped onto the bed and curled his arm around a pillow.

The drug's heady effect was swift to come. His muscles relaxed. His mind quieted. And then darkness fell . . .

The room was silent. Candles burned beside the bed, revealing a fevered brow and the sallow skin of a wraith.

The duke stood beside the window, unmoving, holding back a torrent of immeasurable grief. If the duchess breathed her last breath, that grief would explode. It would be the rebirth of a monster.

"How is she?"

Silence.

"The duke?"

"I fear for his mind. Bring the child."

She can't die, thought Quincy. She can't die. Not again.

"The child is here."

"Open the window," his sister whispered. "I don't want her to sense my death."

James carried the child and kneeled beside the bed.

"Alice, you have a baby brother," said Mirabelle.

"But I'm still squirt."

"Yes, you're still squirt. Bring her closer, James."

The pirate captain rested the child nearer her mother, and she wrapped her arms around the small figure.

"I want you to take care of your brother, Alice."

The girl screwed up her face. "Why, Mama?"

"Because that's what big sisters do."

"I thought that's what nurses do?"

"I'd like you to help nurse. Can you do that for me?"

The child sighed. "Yes."

Mirabelle took in a shaky breath.

"What's wrong, Mama?"

"Nothing's the matter, squirt. I'm just tired."

"It's late," said Alice wisely.

"It is. I'm sorry uncle James had to wake you, but I needed to tell you something . . . I love you, Alice."

"I love you too, Mama."

"Give me a hug and a kiss, squirt."

Alice leaned forward and pecked her mother's lips.

"Take her," said Mirabelle, choking on tears.

James collected his niece and headed for the door. He paused, then retraced his steps and pressed a kiss to his sister's ashen brow before he quit the room, moisture glistening in his eyes.

Once the door was sealed, Mirabelle let out a wretched sob.

No, she can't die, thought Quincy. She can't die. Not again.

"Mirabelle, no! Don't go! Stay, Megan!"

"Quincy."

"I'm sorry. I didn't mean to kill her. Megan, I'm sorry!"

"Quincy, wake up!"

Quincy bolted upright, covered in sweat, his lungs starved for air. In the dimness, he was disoriented, the movement beneath him waves? No, a bed. He was in a strange room but his furniture was the same. Where was the light coming from?

He searched the chamber. A candle. A burning candle. In the hand of a woman.

"Who are you?"

"It's me, Quincy."

Her voice was familiar. He couldn't see her face, so twisted. He rubbed his sore eyes. He was in hell. How much opium had he taken? He couldn't remember. More than usual, though. He couldn't wake up. The nefarious shadows stretched toward him, reaching for him.

"Stay away," he snapped, his breathing ragged. "Don't come near me."

"All right," the feminine voice answered.

The light retreated into the distance. The darkness swallowed him.

"No! Come back," he beseeched.

The light returned.

"It's a dream, Quincy," the gentle voice assured him. "Wake up."

He tried. He grabbed his head, crushing his skull.

The light landed on the bedside table. A warm body settled behind him, and a set of strong yet slender arms reached around his chest and squeezed.

He released his head, spinning with grotesques images and voices, and leaned against the soft and comforting figure, passing out.

Quincy squinted at the bright light. He shut his eyes again, his head throbbing, his limbs trapped, tangled in bedding and some other infernal restraint.

He sighed and shifted his arse when tender fingers stroked his cheek. His eyes shot open, blinded by sunlight, but after a few dazed moments, he focused on the room—and the heavenly body wrapped around him.

He heard a heart pounding beneath his ear, loud and steady beats, like the hypnotic drum of a jungle tribe. A pair of soft breasts cushioned him, while artful hands wandered over his naked back in sensual caresses. As soon as a silky leg slipped between his thighs, Quincy jumped from the bed.

He reeled, his head pulsing, his thoughts mashed and entwined. He couldn't unscramble them and set right what had happened, but when he stared at the woman in his bed — his *wife* — he groaned.

Slowly she sat up, unperturbed, her night rail seductively askew. She wrapped her arms around her raised knees and smiled. "How are you feeling?"

"Like shit!"

Quincy staggered as he grabbed his trousers off the floor and crammed a leg into one of the openings. He trembled at the thought that he'd bedded the wench. And he'd *no* bleedin' memory of it!

"You really have a beautiful arse."

He hardened at the provocative compliment and stuffed his other leg into the breeches before buttoning the flaps.

"What the hell are you doing here?" he demanded, confronting her.

Her long, unfettered tresses, fiery in the morning light, spilled over her shoulders. The green in her eyes glowed bright, like a meadow after a rainfall, while her skin flushed with rose color, making her more beautiful than a nymph — and more tempting than sin.

"Don't you remember?" she asked in a quiet, almost sensitive voice.

No, he didn't remember. He didn't remember a wretched thing!

"The dream?" she prodded.

"What are you talking about? What dream?"

"I heard you from my room, shouting in your sleep. I came to wake you."

"Horseshit."

She had found him intoxicated, under the effects of the opium, and she'd taken advantage of his bloody lust for her.

"You cried for forgiveness," she went on, "and your sister's name, and . . . you also called for another woman."

He chilled.

"Who is Megan?" she whispered.

His heart slammed against his ribs, his legs wavered. He crossed the carpet and grabbed the window frame for support, dazed, sinking into thick, suffocating memories.

Damn you, Holly.

"Megan is my mother." He released a tortured breath. "She died many years ago."

A lifetime ago.

"I also lost my mother," she said softly. "Two years ago. I think of her often."

Was she trying to form a bond with him? Two lost orphans in the world, joining together to create a new family? He shut his eyes again. Their situations were nothing alike. He'd bet his soul she hadn't killed *her* mother.

It was clear the effects of the opium were weakening. Once, the drug had blanketed him in darkness, so thick, not even his nightmares could reach him. But now . . . ? What would he do now?

After a tense pause, he asked, "What do you want from me?"

"To be your wife."

He'd suspected some such rot. "Are you my *wife*?"

"If you mean in body, no. I hope to change that, though."

She was relentless. He would lock his bedroom door in the future.

"I know what you're trying to do," he said roughly. "It won't work."

She slipped off the bed. He heard the sheets rustle before her quiet footfalls approached him, stirring his blood to life.

"What am I trying to do?"

When she reached his backside, he seized. Her lengthy night rail fluttered and whisked against his legs, her hips brushed his thighs, and when her bold fingers traced the curvature of his spine, making him shudder, his breath caught in his throat.

"Are you pregnant?"

Her fingers froze.

He turned and looked into her wide, startled eyes. "Well, Holly? All those men in your little notebook? Did one of them get you pregnant? Is that why you're so intent on a wedding night?"

Her cheeks turned red. Her hand dropped away from his back. "Oh, dear. I see I've made a terrible mistake, trying to make you jealous. I'm afraid I'm not very good at seducing a man."

Oh, hell, she was *too* good at seducing a man, and she didn't even know it! That made her all the more dangerous. And it made her innocent desire for him all the more tempting.

Damn. He almost wished she *was* pregnant. He could deal with the situation then, assure her he'd claim the babe and she needn't take him to bed to secure her reputation and the child's legitimacy.

But Quincy could see in her eyes she wasn't a wanton, that she had never known a lover's touch — and she wanted his to be the first.

"No," he said tightly, restraining his carnal impulses.

She remained silent, contemplating. Her eyes then filled with understanding. "Why?"

"You've already taken too much from me."

Again her fingertips stroked his fevered flesh. "I can give in return."

He flinched at her scorching touch and twisted around, grabbing her wrist, his thumb pressing over her hammering pulse. In a hoarse, strangled voice, he warned, "Do not, Holly."

"But why?" she beseeched, a hope for intimacy burning in her eyes.

"Because I won't forgive you for what you've done." His hand quivered. "I cannot forgive you for creating that painting and taking away my freedom, my life."

"Quincy, I lost my freedom, too. But I want to build a new life — with you."

Hope still burned in her faithful eyes. He had to snuff out that hope.

"You took more than my freedom, Holly, don't you see? You also took away my chance to meet the woman I might truly have loved and married, like one of my brothers."

Her features dropped. A shadow crossed her face. A shadow of bitter regret. And comprehension. He had finally made his sentiment clear: there would be *no* real marriage between them.

She pulled her hand away and retreated one, two

steps before she turned and headed for the door, closing it softly behind her.

CHAPTER 12

Holly smeared the oil paint across the canvas with her hands. She had always painted with a brush and gloves, but she couldn't achieve the effect she now desired with such implements. The tools hindered her efforts to release the emotional wreckage that had run aground in her heart, and she scratched and swirled the mesh of colors: bright ochre and sunset orange, cinnabar red and indigo blue.

Her hands were crusted and stained. Her fingers throbbed. But the nonrepresentational work, the first she had ever produced, captured her dreams and regrets unlike any objective art.

When she slashed the last bit of paint, the layered bursts of color and maddening whirlpools cried out her feelings for her, and she sighed in release.

The floorboards creaked under shifting weight, not her own, though. She grabbed a linen rag and wiped her hands as she turned in the stool and confronted her husband, seated in a chair in the corner of the room.

Her heart expanded, ached in her chest. The blue

of his eyes so closely matched the blue on the canvas, she realized. He was in the turbulent work, wound together with every other sentiment and trial.

"How long have you been watching me?" she asked in a listless voice, her energy spent.

"A few hours. Perhaps more. I don't really know."

His throaty voice sounded almost tender, and she resisted the hope it triggered in her soul. He had made his feelings toward her perfectly clear—he loathed her. She had usurped his life, the act unforgiveable. And her foolish dream of a real and intimate marriage had been shattered like broken glass. All that remained was the possibility of a formal partnership where they might exchange pleasantries over an occasional meal.

She shuddered at the cold reflection. "What are you doing here?"

"I haven't seen you in two days. Emma mentioned you often shut yourself in your studio if you're upset or grieving."

"Did she?" Holly dropped the rag on the table and removed her body apron. Her legs wavered, and she grasped the stool for support. "Well, she misinformed you. I was just distracted with my work. It happens on occasion. I lose sense of the passage of time."

"Have you eaten?"

"I have not. And why do you care?"

His features remained smooth, thoughtful. "I'm not unreasonable, you know?"

Holly approached the sunny window and rotated her stiff shoulders. "I don't know what you mean."

"If you want a lover, take one."

She stiffened. "I beg your pardon?"

"I don't expect you to live without companionship. I'll claim any babes you might have, you needn't fear."

She grabbed the window sill and squeezed the wood until her knuckles turned white. Her belly churned and the impulse to send something flying across the room, preferably toward her husband's "reasonable" head, overwhelmed her. She resisted the urge, though. A fit would not change her grim situation.

"A fair compromise, I suppose," she said without concealing her acrid tone. She returned to the table and doused a rag with turpentine before scrubbing her flesh. "What day is it?"

"Wednesday."

"If you will excuse me, I think I'll rest." After wiping her hands clean, she headed for the door, averting her eyes from Quincy. "I have an engagement with your sister this afternoon."

He queried softly, "Are you going to run to her and cry foul every time we have a disagreement?"

Her heart spasmed. She turned toward her husband, still ensconced in the chair, and neared him until she hovered above his shameless head. "I have an invitation from your sister to help plan Lady Amy's wedding. Fret not, *husband*. I won't betray your disgusting offer to the duchess."

And before losing her remaining poise, Holly stormed from the studio and slammed the door.

~ * ~

"Whatever is the matter, Holly?"

Holly lifted her head and glanced at the other women seated around the table, each holding lace or ribbon or other wedding samples.

"I'm tired, is all," she replied, forcing a smile. "There is nothing the matter."

Sophia snorted beside her. "We all know what they can be like at times."

"They?" asked Holly.

"The Hawkins brothers," said the duchess from across the table. "For all their charms, they can also drive a woman to madness with their stubborn faults."

"Are you sure you'd rather not speak of it?" Amy poured her another cup of tea. "I'm certain we can help."

The ladies were ever so generous and kind, but Holly was convinced they could not repair the brokenness between her and Quincy. She recalled the night he had held her wrist, trembling with grief and disappointment that he had such a wife as *her*.

"Holly, what is it?" Amy thrust a kerchief into her palm. "Tell us, please."

Was she crying? Heavens, how embarrassing. Holly dabbed at her eyes. She'd intended to keep her emotions firmly suppressed, to release them only in the safety of her art studio, but under the ministrations of her sisters-in-law, she'd been unable to restrain her despair. And now, under their concerned expressions, she also couldn't repeat that nothing was the matter.

"We had a dispute," she said instead, keeping to the truth without revealing any of the crude details.

"I don't know how to resolve it, though."

"Hmm." Sophia picked up a pin and a square of ivory satin. "Whenever James and I have a dispute, we play a game."

Holly pinched her brows together. "A game?"

"A game of chess." She stabbed the square of fabric with the pin. "Loser pays a forfeit."

An intriguing thought. Holly wondered, "What sort of forfeit?"

"Absolute submission—usually in bed."

Holly felt her cheeks warm, but the other women chuckled.

"I invite Edmund to dinner and have a hardy meal prepared," said Amy with a sly smile. "He loves food. Once he's devoured the fare, the disputed matter is usually forgiven or forgotten."

"So you see," said Mirabelle. "Each one of my brother's has a weakness to be exploited. I'm sure you'll find Quincy's and settle the matter soon. Give it a little more time. You're newlyweds, my dear."

Their candor was welcomed, but unhelpful, thought Holly. Her trouble with Quincy stemmed from herself. *She* was the disputed matter. How to play a game or prepare a meal that would make her husband forget he had *not* married the woman of his dreams?

Holly considered carrying the hurtful secret in private for the rest of her married life, but she also considered the burden of doing such a thing. The crushing weight would destroy her one day, she was sure.

In a small voice, she admitted, "He will not forgive me."

Amy cupped her hand. "Forgive you, Holly? For what?"

Her heart cramped and she heaved a giant breath. "I am not like the rest of you," she whispered. "I'm a notorious artist with a sordid past. Quincy had hoped to find and marry a better woman, like his brothers before him."

The ladies around the table exchanged silent glances, and Holly instantly regretted her confession. She had placed the women in the awkward positions of both agreeing with her husband and still comforting her.

Holly attempted to excuse herself when Sophia grabbed her other hand in an unbreakable hold, keeping her from moving an inch.

"Should we tell her?" the exotic beauty asked.

"I believe so," returned Amy.

Mirabelle remained quiet, reflective. "It's too dangerous."

"I would hardly think so," countered Sophia. "If she ever tells another living soul, we'll confess her identity as Lord H. I don't believe she'd ever risk such scandalous exposure, not with a teenage sister to marry off."

Holly balked. Were the women about to *blackmail* her? Heavens, whatever for? What had she done to deserve such iniquitous treatment?

Oh, why hadn't she remained silent about her troubles with her husband? She should not have confessed such intimate details to his family, clearly. It was wholly improper. And she would pay for her folly by suffering under the threat of extortion!

The duchess finally nodded in agreement. Her

umber eyes fell on Holly. "We all have a past, my dear."

Holly twisted her hand, trying to free herself from Sophia, but the woman clamped down even harder.

"It's all right," Holly rushed to express before any more uneasy confessions were revealed. "I should not have bothered you with my private concerns."

"You are always welcome to come to me with your concerns, Holly."

"And to me," said Sophia.

Amy smiled. "And to me."

"We are sisters," the duchess resumed, "and we support one another."

"Always," said Sophia and Amy in unison.

Holly blinked. Were they going to blackmail her or initiate her into a sisterhood? She stopped struggling and listened with intent.

"Who am I?" asked Sophia. "Where have I come from?"

Under the woman's darkening gaze, Holly quivered. "You are an heiress from the West Indies. Your late father, an Englishman, and your late mother, a Portuguese lady, owned a plantation on the island of Jamaica."

Sophia lifted a cunning brow. "It does sound very respectable, does it not? In truth, I am the daughter of a pirate and a whore. I was raised in a brothel until the age of twelve when my mother insisted I earn my keep on my back. I refused and left her to live with my mad father in the jungle. After his death, I took his stolen riches and came to England."

Holly dropped her jaw. "You . . . You are not . . ."

"Telling the truth?" A wicked light sparkled in

her bay brown eyes. "Oh, but I am."

Holly believed her then. Her sophisticated ensemble belied the dangerous, even venomous tone in her voice—a tone no proper miss could ever wield.

Hesitant, Holly turned toward Lady Amy. "Are you the daughter of a duke and duchess?"

"I am." She angled her head, her golden curls bobbing. "But as a child, I was abducted by Gravenhurst."

"Your former husband?"

"Yes," she said in a low voice. "You see, my father had wronged the marquis, terribly so, and in revenge, Gravenhurst had taken me away from my family. I escaped into the rookeries before he could kill me and found sanctuary in a foundling asylum."

"Goodness," breathed Holly, captivated by the unfolding account.

"I eventually found work in a notorious house called the Pleasure Palace, where I danced in disguise as the foreign princess, Zarsiti, enticing rich men to part with their gold coins."

Holly's jaw remained in position this time as she grew accustomed to the fantastical tales. She next peeked at Mirabelle under lowered lashes. "I'm not even going to guess your past, Your Grace."

The duchess chuckled. "I was raised by my father and brothers. My mother died from childbed fever shortly after giving birth to Quincy."

Holly gasped. Quincy had shouted his mother's name in his troubled sleep, she remembered. And he had begged the woman for forgiveness. Forgiveness for what, though?

"My father was pressed into navel service when James and William were just boys," she went on. "Stolen from his family without the chance to even say farewell, he remained imprisoned aboard the naval vessel for ten years. He was treated heinously during that time, so when the naval vessel was attacked by pirates, my father turned traitor and joined the pirate crew. He sailed the Caribbean for two years under the pirate captain, Dawson."

"My father," added Sophia.

"Yes." Mirabelle smiled. "Dawson saved my father from the brutal life of a pressed seaman. Soon the two men became friends, and Dawson released my father from service with his fair share of the booty. Finally, my father returned home. Reunited with my mother, they had three more children, and my father took to piracy as a career. He purchased a schooner, named it the *Bonny Meg* after my mother, and raided the high seas for many years before he grew ill and handed command of the vessel over to my eldest brother, James."

Holly's eyes widened. "James is a pirate?"

"Was a pirate," corrected Sophia. "He once roamed the waves as Black Hawk."

"What?" cried Holly. "*The* infamous rogue?"

His wife smiled with pride. "The very one."

"He's retired, though," assured Mirabelle. "All of my brothers are retired from piracy."

"Well, that's . . . Wait." Holly almost toppled from her chair. "*All* of your brothers? You mean . . . ?"

"Yes, even Quincy."

"My husband is a pirate?"

"A former pirate," reiterated Amy. "We're all

married—or soon-to-be married—to one."

"I am the only exception," from Mirabelle. "I married the reformed 'Duke of Rogues.' *He* is the one married to a former pirate."

"*You* are a pirate!"

"Shhh," hissed the duchess. "Not so loud, Holly. I don't want my children to hear the truth. They're troublesome sprites, as is. Imagine if they caught word their mother was once a pirate? They'd turn into veritable hobgoblins."

Holly heaved a deep breath. Her head was spinning with too many sensational tales. The family had accepted her into the fold *because* of her scandalous past, not in spite of it? Pirates attended high society balls, masquerading as gentlemen?

But one pertinent question remained after all the shocking confessions.

"Who am I, then?" asked Holly.

"A woman with a past?" suggested Amy.

"Just like one of us," offered Sophia.

"Family," said Mirabelle with a soft smile. "So don't think for one moment Quincy is looking for a 'better' lady. If he wants to be with the same sort of woman as one of his brothers, he's already with her."

Holly sighed. She even simpered. For the first time in many black days, hope sprouted in her heart. Her husband might be furious with her for the way in which they had married, madcap and under duress, but in time, might he really grow to care for her?

CHAPTER 13

Y ou look like hell," said James, straddling a chair.

Captain James Hawkins was the last of the brothers to arrive at the pub. Not since their bachelors days, when they'd all sailed aboard the *Bonny Meg*, had the four found time to spend together and get pissed.

"I feel like hell," growled Quincy. He sensed a familiar, uncomfortable pressure on his chest as he remembered his wife's impudent condemnation. A disgusting offer, was it? Fine. If she wanted to be a martyr and remain celibate, she could go right ahead. He sure as hell wasn't going to maintain a monastic life. And he would *not* feel guilty about avoiding his "husbandly" duty.

"I was talking to Will, pup."

"Oh." Quincy rolled his eyes toward William. "He's looked like that for months."

James shouted for ale, then, "What's the matter, Will?"

After downing a pint, William wiped his mouth. "Nothing's the matter." He slammed the empty glass on the table and belched.

The brothers exchanged bewildered glances, for William *never* imbued.

James shrugged, taking a swig of malt. There was a time when he would've beat the confessions out of them. But he'd considerably mellowed since his marriage to Sophia.

He turned toward Quincy next. "So what the devil's wrong with you?"

"Forget I said anything." Quincy raised his mug. "We're here for a toast. To Eddie and Amy."

The others lifted their hands. "Eddie and Amy."

A cacophony of striking glass filled the already noisy pub.

"Any word on Gravenhurst?" asked James.

"No." Edmund squeezed his tankard. "The bastard's still at large."

"I don't want to dampen your good fortune, but have you considered he might try to ruin the wedding? Or come back to hurt Amy?"

"Consider it? It's all I bloody think about, protecting Amy. If I can't stand outside her parent's house, I send patrols to guard her."

"And the wedding day?"

"I'll have runners at the church and during the ball, looking out for him."

"We'll keep watch, too," said James, his voice lethal.

Whatever their differences or disputes, the brothers always protected their family.

A sardonic grin soon crossed the pirate captain's face as he turned his attention back toward his youngest brother. "How's married life, pup?"

"Fine," gritted Quincy.

"Trouble in paradise already?"

"Whoever said it was paradise?"

Edmund snorted. "Can't keep the wife happy? And you, the charmer in the family?"

"Piss off. All of you."

James and Edmund sniggered. William called for another round.

"It's a strange time, indeed," said James, still chuckling, "when *mine* is the only uncomplicated life."

"Perhaps it's the full moon," grumbled Quincy.

"A word of advice to you all."

"Oh, crikey," groaned Edmund.

But James ignored the protest and lifted his mug once more. "Whatever your troubles, men, heed the wise words of our forerunner Blackbeard, 'damnation seize my soul if I give you quarters, or take any from you'."

The brothers knocked glasses again. But Quincy considered James's counsel *the* worst he had ever heard. He imagined the position he was in and what it would mean to take up such advice—both refusing to surrender *and* refusing to accept surrender from Holly. A fight to the death, in other words. Gads! Was his brother mad or foxed? Quincy *wanted* his wife's capitulation. He'd remain miserable until then.

The brothers quit the pub after some more ribald talk. William was so thoroughly drunk by the end of the night, James and Edmund had to carry him home. Quincy also treaded home on foot, though his gait slowed as he stepped onto Park Street and stalled altogether when he reached his house.

Was he going to pussyfoot every time he arrived home? Like hell! He'd set his wife straight on the matter of their marriage once and for all: that they would lead separate, private lives. He with his lovers. And she with hers — or not. He didn't much care at that point. He just wanted peace between them.

Quincy pounded on the front door until his disapproving butler opened the barrier.

"Where's my wife?" he demanded, his words slightly slurred.

The old man frowned before announcing, "In the studio, sir."

Quincy dismissed the disagreeable servant and climbed the stairs, heading for the studio. At the door, he paused and inhaled a fortifying breath. He then entered the room without making a sound.

Inside, Holly was seated on a stool, covered in a body apron, her luscious locks pinned in an untidy bun, loose wisps sweeping across her temple and neck. He watched her furious fingers, stained with charcoal, gouge the canvas with a flurry of black marks, and for a moment he remained enthralled. Again, she didn't notice his appearance. Again, he had the opportunity to study her in surreptitious solitude.

He considered interrupting her work, to resolve the tense matter between them, but instead he found himself seated in an armchair in the corner of the room. And again, he leaned his head against the backrest, observing her as she brought to life another piece of art.

It had startled him, the depth of her talent. He had thought her work limited to tawdry nudes, but since retiring as Lord H, Holly had unleashed an otherworldly ability.

He shifted his gaze to her previous work, the oil drying on an easel, swirling with abundant color. He was lost in the never-ending whirlpool of brilliant strokes. He captured splatters of blue and red and yellow paint: colors of passionate emotions. Anger. Hurt. Lust. Hope. All screamed at him. And he grimaced in pain.

Quincy shut his eyes and envisioned her slender fingers smoothing the conflicting hues, digging through them, blending them together, then slashing them apart. More paint. Heavy, thick, emotive color. Soon peace emerged as the fractious pigments joined in harmony.

At last.

He sighed. He needed those slender fingers to do the same to him, to smooth and dig and blend and slash until his shattered soul was remade in unified fragments.

Quincy opened his eyes, the world still spinning like the artwork. What rot! He was sloshed. And he tended to make an ass of himself whenever he was drunk. Perhaps now wasn't the right time to talk with his wife.

He was about to leave the room when Holly sniffed the air. Her concentration shattered, she looked over her shoulder and her flushed features and breathless beauty punched him straight in the gut. She had a smudge of charcoal across her fine jaw, and he had an insatiable desire to wipe away the soot with his thumb.

He really was an ass. He shouldn't have entered the room when he hadn't full control of his senses. He barely made it through one of their encounters when he *had* his wits together.

"I smell liquor." She made a moue. "Were you at a gentlemen's club?"

He snorted. "A pub. I don't play the bleedin' nob when there's no lady fussing about."

She humphed and returned to her sketch, but her shoulders soon slumped. "I shall have to finish it another time." She looked back at him, piqued. "What are you doing here?"

"It's my house," he growled at her audacious reproach. "I can sit in any damn room that pleases me."

Her brows arched. "It pleases you to sit in here? With that?" She pointed toward a draped canvas, his nude. "And me?"

Quincy scowled. He hadn't meant to suggest he enjoyed her company, that he was looking for more than an orderly, unfeeling marriage.

"Shit," he hissed, reproaching himself for his folly. He pushed out of the chair and headed for the door. "I think I'll go to that gentlemen's club, after all. I need a good bedding."

"I suppose I shouldn't expect more from a pirate."

He hardened. Every bone in his body. Stone. Cold. Dead.

"What?" he rasped.

"Isn't that all pirates do? Pillage and whore?"

Slowly he turned around, blood throbbing through his veins, and met her bold stare. "What the devil did you call me?"

She quirked another brow. "A pirate. Or do you prefer cutthroat? Blackguard? What is the most appropriate term?"

Quincy couldn't believe his ears. How the hell had she discovered his past identity? His heart hammered, and he sensed himself being pushed into a corner. But he quickly remembered he was privy to *her* secret identity. She wouldn't dare breathe a word about his piracy and hurt his family, not when he could destroy her. So what was she doing taunting him?

Holly hopped off the stool and reached for a rag, wiping her grimy fingers. "Well, I shan't keep you from your whore."

She strutted toward the door, and as she passed him, he grabbed a hold of her arm. Slowly he pulled her across the breadth of his chest until she was positioned in front of him. He glared at her. She lifted her chin, undaunted, and returned his stare. Something kindled in her bright green eyes. Humor? Anger? Hope? What the deuces was she thinking?

"How?" he growled.

"How do I know you're a pirate? I have my source."

"Tell me."

"No."

Her flat refusal disarmed him. Damn her! *Who* had told her about his past? He had to plug the leak before others discovered the truth, as well.

"You *will* tell me," he gritted through clenched teeth.

"I don't see how," she quipped. "Unless . . ."

"Unless what?" he snapped.

"I propose a trade."

"I won't bed you."

His swift refusal turned her delicate features into ominous storm clouds. "I wasn't going to ask you to 'bed' me."

His heartbeat steadied at the assertion. "Then what do you want, wench?"

"A kiss."

"No."

"And not a peck on the cheek," she resumed as if he hadn't just denied the request. "You once welcomed my artistic study." Her voice dropped to a seductive octave. "You once offered me the opportunity to take my hands and lips and study you until I was satisfied. Well, I'm accepting the invitation. And *then* I will tell you my source."

He stiffened at her proposed "trade." His blood burned in anticipation of her downright extortion — and the pleasure he would feel in giving her what she demanded: a bloody kiss that could ruin him.

Quincy girded his muscles as his brain flooded with memories of that night in his coach, and he knew, he just knew he wasn't strong enough to resist her, not when he was drunk *and* in need of a woman's touch.

He shut his eyes, about to refuse her again, when she offered:

"I want just a kiss, I promise." She whispered, "I won't take more than that."

He had to be a bloody fool to trust *her* with keeping the kiss from becoming a thorough bedding, but what other choice did he have? He wasn't going to lock her in the studio and starve her until she confessed her source. He even shuddered at the violent image. He would never hurt a woman, much less Holly. It seemed there was no other way to get what he wanted except to charm his conniving wife.

He said not a word. Instead, he lifted his thumb to her jaw line and smoothed away the charcoal smudge. At first, she appeared confused. But as the silence stretched between them and he stroked her soft skin more and more, her eyes widened in understanding.

A glow spread across her cheeks. Her breathing slowed, deepened.

"Sit," she bade him.

A tremor wracked him before he dropped back into the armchair and waited.

CHAPTER 14

Holly maintained a distance from her husband, breath trapped in her throat. A part of her had expected his outright refusal at her proposal. Another part of her had hoped . . .

Well, she had her wish. A real kiss.

The pressure on her lungs was so great, she finally released a long, measured breath. Her heart thumped, deafening drumbeats in her ears. The room warmed with unbearable heat, and she removed her leather apron. Still flushed, she pulled the fasteners from her knotted hair, allowing the tresses to tumble free.

Quincy watched her every movement, his eyes dark pools of swirling emotions, and his riveting stare twisted the already tight muscles in her belly. Raking her bottom lip with her teeth, she wondered what she should do next, but he offered her no guidance, remaining silent and unmoving in the chair.

Her gaze flitted toward his hands, his fingers digging into the armrests, and she felt the same restless energy, the same nervous want.

She took a bold step toward him and heard his quickened breath. As her own pulse pounded, she approached him again and nestled between his splayed thighs.

The man's hot breath now bathed her, and she closed her eyes, reveling in the intimacy. She loved to feel his presence, to just listen to his fevered intake and exhale of air. She only missed his touch.

Holly remembered the night she'd held her husband in her arms, after his disturbing dream had departed and only peaceful rest remained, their hearts beating in unison. She would have that moment again, she thought with shivering delight. And this time, he would share the erotic moment with her.

Her eyes fluttered open and she met his still fiery stare. Heavens, he was beautiful. Blood swelled in her veins as she slowly lowered herself into his lap.

His muscular legs flinched, as if she'd scorched him, and she gasped at the almost electric spark that snapped between them. Her quivering hand went to his chest, cradled the muscle above his rampant heart, and she matched the thundering beats.

His hand clamped hard over hers, and the smoldering look in his eyes now held an air of uncertainty. Quickly, before he reneged on their agreement, she wrapped her arms around his neck and took his mouth between her lips with savage hunger.

Sweet heaven!

Holly moaned like a wanton wench. A kiss from him was every bit as wonderful as she remembered, but her nerves still thrummed with violent need.

"Touch me," she begged in a hoarse whisper, breaking from the kiss for one desperate breath.

He flexed his muscles in resistance.

"Touch me. Please." She skimmed her tongue over his sensuous lips. "Just one touch."

His guttural groan vibrated down her throat. It wasn't long before trembling fingers stroked her spine and fingernails scraped the back of her head, pressing her deeper into the kiss.

Yes, she cried in her soul, rolling her lips in ravenous want. Her skin burst with gooseflesh, and as her husband met her fervor thrust for thrust, as their bodies moistened with sweat and undulated in a harmonious rhythm, she knew one kiss would never be enough.

An inconsolable pain suddenly ripped through her. The ache swelled inside her and screamed for satisfaction, an unimaginable longing for more, and tears filled her eyes. The briny drops spilled down her cheeks and into her mouth, into his mouth.

"Jesus, Holly."

His prayer sounded so sincere, beseeching the strength to resist her. Why couldn't he forgive her? Why couldn't he let go of the past and seize the future? Seize her?

He pushed her away.

"Are you satisfied?" he gasped, his chest heaving, his body shuddering.

She grazed his mussed hair with her fingertips. How she yearned to hear him call her "sweet" again, to feel him breathe the endearment against her naked flesh as he tasted her body like a husband should. "I will never be satisfied until I have you inside me."

Another groan. A plaintive, even painful groan as his erection throbbed against her thigh.

"I want you," she whispered into his downturned ear. "I will always want you—and no other."

She nipped his earlobe with her teeth, smothered his temple with another sultry buss before she moved off his lap.

A pang of regret squeezed her breast the moment she separated from him, and an impotent want filled her. She should not have asked for the kiss without the assurance of *real* fulfillment. One kiss from her husband was not enough. It would never be enough.

But she had learned that lesson too late.

"A promise is a promise," she said, breathless, meeting his haggard gaze. "Your sister."

He stared at her, bemused. "What?"

"Your sister is my source. She told me about your past as a pirate."

And with that revelation, Holly headed for the door, her steps faltering.

His sister?

His bleedin' sister?

Quincy shut his eyes. He was stiff, suffering from unslaked lust. And for what? He had discovered his *sister* was a bloody gossip!

What the hell had he done? Holly had left her mark on him with her lips, her teeth, her salacious tongue. She had explored and pillaged and branded him hers, renting from him every ounce of resistance. He had no fight left in him. His body raged for satisfaction. And he knew no other woman would gratify him like his wife. He also realized the next time he confronted her, he would give in to her wiles. He would give her her blasted wedding night.

Quincy reeled as he left the chair. He could smell her on him, taste her tears in his mouth. Tears? Why had she cried? She had begged for his touch. Had he hurt her?

I will never be satisfied until I have you inside me.

Aye, he had hurt her. His body hurt, too, demanded release. He had struggled against her for far too long, allowing his desire for her to grow stronger. He had approached the matter all wrong. He understood now that time wouldn't lessen a thing. If he wanted to untangle himself from his wife's bewitching grip, he had to surrender to his lust.

"Shit."

He hated to lose.

The charcoal sketch on the easel suddenly captured his notice. As he neared the dark, whirling strokes, a remarkable image appeared. He dropped in the stool and stared at the portrait of Holly. Was this how she saw herself?

His fingers traced the lines of her face. She had reproduced her aesthetics, her proportions and symmetries. But the work was more than an anatomical study. There was a wild beauty about her. There was also an unmistakable melancholy. The shadows behind her loomed and threatened her. Her eyes looked off the canvas, as if searching for someone . . .

Quincy pulled his hand away. Was she looking for him?

His heart thudded at the notion that she both wanted *and* needed him, and he stumbled away from the stool as if he'd witnessed a wraith. He found his head spinning with the thought of giving her everything she asked for, and of taking everything she offered him.

I can give in return.

Could she? Could she give him . . . ?

No, it was a stupid dream. He would never find peace. Not with Holly.

Quincy stormed from the studio and headed for his room. He turned up the gaslight and ransacked the chest at the foot of his bed, searching for the satchel of opium. When he found it, he tore apart the drawstrings and dumped all the sugar-coated capsules into his palm.

He crushed the capsules in his trembling fist. His soul screamed for the drug. His heart begged him not to take it, to take the offer Holly had made him instead.

But he was sweating, his heart pounding, and the paste in his hand promised him an immediate remedy from the demons that would never be exorcised.

Quincy swallowed all the capsules. It wasn't long before a heavy, blissful sleep draped over him and he collapsed on the bed, blacking out . . .

He opened his eyes as morning light entered the room and spread across the bed. The white light formed a fine line over a woman's slumbering profile. It caressed her throat and travelled down her chest and across the peaks of her naked breasts.

She stirred under the warm light, turned her head

116

away from it. Her lashes fluttered, her dreamy green eyes appeared – and she smiled.

His chest ached under the spell of her brilliant smile, more brilliant than the white light. A hand reached for him and stroked his temple, his cheek, and he sighed at the soothing touch. But when a finger traced the contours of his mouth, a simmering heat stirred in his belly.

"Good morning," she whispered.

He was strapped for breath, for words. She rolled over him, her red hair spilling around him, sheltering him. Her smile never weakened. She brushed his chin with her thumb before her mouth covered his in a sensual kiss.

When he opened his eyes again, her beautiful smile remained. Beams of light pierced her hair and flashed across her brow and nose. He wrapped his arms around her back, holding her tight.

"Don't wake up," she said. "Don't ever wake up."

Quincy leaned over the side of the bed and retched into the chamber pot. He gasped for air, his lungs cramped and starved. His body spasmed, contorted with pain. He pulled in breath after torturous breath. The room rocked back and forth, and he retched again. Finally, he groaned, and rolled back onto the bed, slinging an arm over his pounding brow.

He had stopped breathing. Why?

Opium. He had taken opium, he remembered. A lot of opium. If he had taken a capsule more, he'd be dead.

Don't ever wake up.

He had missed his chance to be at peace. He would have stayed in that moment, in that light.

Forever.

With her.

"Quincy!"

A voice hollered. A door burst open. Hands grabbed his shirt collar, shaking him.

"Wake up!"

Quincy choked, "I'm awake."

The hands loosened, then released him. He rolled to the side of the bed and sat up, rubbing his burning eyes, then gasped and sputtered when water knocked him in the face. Hard.

"Get up!" screamed the voice. "I need you."

"I said I was awake!" he roared and opened his groggy eyes. His heart almost stopped again when he found Holly standing a few feet away from him in her night rail, the whites of her eyes filled with tiny red veins, a pitcher in her hands—her bloody hands.

He went numb.

"Holly." He bounded to his feet, reeled, then steadied. He rent the pitcher from her trembling grip, setting it aside, then grabbed her blood-soaked fingers, searching for the injury. "Where are you hurt?" he demanded. "Tell me."

"It isn't me," she cried. "It's Emma. She's dying."

"What?" he rasped, his mind twisting and turning in disorientation.

"Hurry!" she shouted, then bolted from the room.

He staggered after her.

CHAPTER 15

Quincy trailed his wife by a few meters. When she reached her sister's bedroom door and released a wretched sob, a knowing dread entered his belly.

He quickly followed her inside the chamber — and his heart seized. Air swirled in his lungs with nowhere to escape.

Emma was on the bed, pale, shivering and moaning, holding her midriff in obvious pain, but the pool of blood around her was enormous; it filled the bed.

Quincy was unprepared for the vomit in his belly. It climbed up his windpipe, making him choke, and he swallowed the bile before stumbling closer to the bed.

Holly rushed to her sibling's side and grasped the girl's hand. "Do something," she pleaded with him. "I can't stop the bleeding."

His mind filled with gruesome memories of the night his own sister had suffered through childbirth, and a pressure came over his chest, squeezing his lungs, until he finally released the breath he was holding.

"Summon a doctor," he ordered.

"She'll bleed to death by the time he arrives," cried Holly. "You're a ship's surgeon. Can't you stop the hemorrhage?"

Aye, he was a ship's surgeon, and he could sew a gash or even amputate a leg, but stop a woman from hemorrhaging? He just didn't know how to do that.

"Quincy!"

Her holler jostled him. He rubbed his burning eyes and shook his head, still wet with water, before he approached the bed and leaned forward, palpating Emma's belly.

The girl groaned when he touched her lower abdomen. He frowned.

"What is it?" asked Holly. "Is she having her menses? No, of course not. There's too much blood."

"Aye," he whispered, thoughtful. "Too much blood." There was only one other cause for her bleeding, he reasoned. Softly he stroked the girl's temple. "Emma, can you hear me?"

Teeth chattering, Emma nodded.

"What did you take, Emma?" he probed, his voice calm.

"Take what?" demanded his wife, her features contorted in anguish. "What's happening to her, Quincy? Tell me!"

He met her wide-eyed gaze. "She's having an abortion."

Holly's jaw dropped. "That's . . . impossible. She's never been with a man. She doesn't know anything about procreation. You're wrong."

"I don't think I'm wrong, Holly."

"You're wrong," she insisted.

She wasn't prepared to accept the truth, but she was right about one thing: her sister would bleed to death if he didn't do something.

Quincy shut off his emotions like the turn of a switch. He had learned how to do that long ago when in the heat of battle, displacing his fears and doubts, warring with skill and instinct alone.

"I need hot water," he instructed. "Clean towels. And shepherd's purse."

Gathering her flustered features, Holly bobbed her head. "There's some in the culinary garden."

"Good. And fetch my medical books. They're in my room, along with my surgical bag."

Holly wiped her tear-stained face with the back of her hand, smearing a bit of blood across her cheek, before hurrying toward the door.

Quincy overheard her issuing orders to the servants who'd gathered in the passageway, likely having caught the commotion.

Alone in the room with Emma, he repeated softly, "What did you take, Emma?"

"P-pennyroyal."

He chilled. "Oh, Emma, how much did you take?"

The herb had been used for centuries as an abortifacient, but if too much was ingested, or if the essential oil was downed, the herb became toxic, even poisonous.

"I-I don't know," she stuttered.

Quincy cursed under his breath. If the blood loss didn't end her life, the pennyroyal might.

He ran his fingers through his mussed hair and

shut his still fevered eyes, taking a fortifying breath. He couldn't let her die like his sister had almost died, like his mother had died. He had to improvise, and he rummaged through his muddled memories, searching for a solution.

Soon Holly returned with her maid. The two women set everything on the writing desk.

Quincy pushed aside his remaining reservation and approached the table. He opened his anatomy text to the female form and laid out the page on reproductive organs. He then dipped his hands in the bowl of hot water and dried them in a clean towel.

He had also studied pagan herbal medicine and had learned hot water, for whatever reason, increased a patient's chance of survival. He would use every bit of knowledge he possessed, superstitious and all, to try and save the girl.

"Open my surgical bag," he instructed Holly.

Her fingers trembling, she unstrapped the leather buckles.

Quincy sifted through the instruments and retrieved the clamp forceps. He placed the tweezers-like implement into the water, as well, before he stripped a few leaves from the shepherd's purse.

"Here." He handed Holly the herb. "Have her swallow these."

Holly rushed to her sister's bedside and coaxed her to open her mouth. "There now, Emma. Swallow. That's a good dear."

As Holly fed her sister the leaves, Quincy stripped the rest of the shepherd's purse, an idea having formed in his mind, and balled the herb into a cork-size bundle, tying it together with a piece of the stem. He retrieved the clamp forceps from the bowl of water and gripped the herbal cluster between the pinchers.

Holly wondered, "What will that do?"

"Stop the bleeding, I hope."

"But how?"

"The herb constricts the veins. I've used it to stop bleeding wounds in the past."

If a skin injury wouldn't clot, the shepherd's purse, laid over the wound, stemmed the blood flow, and while Emma didn't have a laceration, he prayed the herb would still work and restrict the bleeding.

He briefly studied the page on a woman's uterus, heaved a giant breath, then walked toward the bed. "I need to insert the herb."

Holly's cheeks, moist from tears, turned bright red, but she quickly nodded and crawled onto the blood-stained bed, wrapping her arms around her sister's quivering shoulders.

The old maid stepped forward. "I've delivered a babe or two in my time," she quipped. "I'll hold the girl's legs."

"Thank you," he said, relieved for the help.

Holly averted her eyes and pressed her lips to her sister's brow, murmuring soothing words. The old maid removed a blood-soaked towel from under Emma's night rail, then positioned the girl's legs as if preparing her for a birthing.

Emma sobbed in pain or fright or mortification, Quincy wasn't sure, and he swiftly set to work, slipping the herbal concoction inside her.

The girl cried out and clamped her muscles,

stymieing his progress. He could feel the sweat across his brow. His own fingers trembled as he forced the shepherd's purse deeper toward her womb. Reaching the clamp forceps's limit, he released the herb and withdrew the instrument.

Quickly the old maid covered Emma with a blanket. "There now," she cooed. "It's all over."

But it wasn't over, he thought darkly, wiping his brow with his forearm. Would the herb control the hemorrhage? And what about the pennyroyal she'd ingested? Would it take her life?

He staggered back, unsteady on his feet, still feeling the sedate and dizzying effects of the opium. He dropped the bloody instrument into the bowl of water and washed his hands again. There was nothing more he could do but wait. And pray. Pray the girl survived. Pray he hadn't made a mistake — and caused another woman's death.

CHAPTER 16

In the quiet room, under the warm glow of lamplight, Holly watched her sister sleep. The hemorrhage had finally come to a surcease, and Quincy had removed the shepherd's purse. Even so, Emma had lost a lot of blood. And Holly waited with baited breath for the girl to recover.

It was half past three in the morning, but she was too afraid to close her eyes. What if something terrible happened to Emma while she slumbered?

Holly looked over her shoulder instead and studied her husband, reclined in an armchair on the other side of the room. His eyes half shut, she wasn't sure if he was gazing at her or having a waking dream.

A welter of feelings stormed her breast. Gratitude. Anger. Confusion. What had happened to him tonight? Why hadn't he roused when she'd cried for his help?

She reflected on the heart-stopping moment she'd realized her sister was in peril, when the blood had flowed and flowed without end. She'd had to leave her dying kin unattended while she'd fetched

Quincy. And when she'd reached his room, he still wouldn't wake. She'd had to shake him, dumped water over him. Holly had never seen him so lifeless. Was he ill?

And he hadn't revived upon entering Emma's room. She'd had to shout at him to do something before her sister perished in her arms.

Holly heaved a trembling breath. In the shadows, Quincy looked ever so forbidding. She was suddenly unsure about him, about the strange spell that had come over him. But it wasn't the right time to broach the disturbing matter.

Her thoughts returned to Emma and more unsettling emotions rattled in her chest. If she hadn't been so flustered by her earlier kiss with Quincy, she would never have paced her room in frustration or heard the whimpering sounds coming from her sister's room next door. The girl would have died alone and in pain. She still might . . .

Holly pushed aside her heavy reflections. She wouldn't dwell on the macabre. Emma was young and strong. She would live. She had to.

Emma stirred. "Holly?"

"I'm here, dear." She pushed out of her chair and climbed onto the clean bed. "Rest."

"Holly," her voice cracked, "I'm sorry."

"Oh, Emma."

Holly couldn't deny it any longer. She had failed to protect her sister. Too distracted by her marital troubles, she'd allowed a villain to take advantage of the vulnerable girl.

She embraced Emma. "I am at fault, not you. I failed to look after you, as proper."

And she would never forgive herself for such a shameful mistake.

"You did nothing wrong, Holly. I—"

"No, dear. I am at fault. And I will make it right. Who did this to you? Who hurt you, Emma?"

She wanted the blackguard's head. He had seduced an innocent adolescent, then abandoned her with child. He deserved an eternity in hell!

"I—I—" Emma broke into sobs.

"No, don't cry. You must regain your strength. Shhh. Everything will be better in the morning."

Soon the girl calmed and drifted back to sleep.

Holly sighed, her arms still locked around her sister's shoulders. She wouldn't press the girl for answers, not until she had healed . . . if she healed.

A shudder went through her. First her father had died, then her mother. She had a husband, but not a marriage partner. And to lose Emma because . . .

Her throat filled with bitter tears. Slowly she separated from her sister. As the tears fell, Holly slipped off the bed and paced the rug, restless with regret and fear.

"You are not at fault," came a deep voice from the shadows.

Her shoulders quivering, she turned toward her husband. "Then who is at fault?" she whispered. "It is my duty to protect Emma until she marries."

"It is *our* duty to protect her," he returned. "She is my sister, too."

An overpowering awareness came over her, making her gasp for breath. Another man might have tossed her sister from the house for becoming pregnant out of wedlock. A truly cruel man might even have let her bleed to death, citing it just punishment for sin. But not her husband. He considered Emma family. He considered *her* family.

Something changed inside Holly at that moment. The sentiment rooted itself in her heart with a frighteningly iron hold.

Her tears poured. Quincy moved away from the armchair, his eyes sharp with intent. When he reached her, he slipped his palms across her cheeks. Air trapped in her lungs. Without a word, he pressed his lips against her mouth.

Holly released her breath, then dragged in another. Her heart thudded, her blood roared in her ears, but his kiss wasn't borne of passion, rather something more. It soothed the soul. In every way, his tender touch eased her grief and offered her hope.

Her fingers trembling, she reached for his face. She stroked his skin, rough with stubble, and returned his buss with an earnest want for true intimacy . . . that of two connected hearts.

"Rest," he breathed over her lips, ending the healing kiss. "Everything will be better in the morning," he echoed her own words.

And she believed him.

When a gentle hand rocked her shoulder, Holly opened her heavy eyes. She focused on the cloudy figure hovering above her and soon recognized her sister-in-law, the Duchess of Wembury.

Oh, no. She had fallen asleep!

Holly tossed the blanket aside and jumped from the armchair. "Emma!"

"Shhh," whispered Mirabelle. "The girl is fine."

Holly darted toward the bed and found her sister pale, but alive and soundly slumbering. Lady Amy was tucking the covers around her, while Sophia mopped the girl's brow with a cool compress.

Holly slumped her aching shoulders with relief.

"Get some rest," encouraged Mirabelle, stroking her spine. "We'll look after the girl."

With such attentive ladies at her sister's bedside, Holly left the room, grateful for their support. Her legs wavered as she trudged through the passageway toward her own room, but she first stopped at Quincy's door. He must have sent word to his kin about Emma. She wanted to thank him for that. But she also wanted to make sure he was all right. She still didn't know what had caused his dissociative state last night.

Quietly she opened the door.

Ensconced in an armchair, Quincy stared out the window. She hadn't seen him since he had kissed her with such healing tenderness. Her heart thumped with quickened beats as she approached the bed and settled on the feather tick.

Something had changed between them after the kiss. A bond had formed. He'd offered her solace during one of the worst moments of her life. She would offer him the same if he desired. She hoped he desired her help. It would mean he trusted her. It would mean the start of a new relationship. The one she had longed for since their wedding day.

"Quincy?"

Slowly he turned and gazed at her, his deep blue eyes smoldering. A warmth filled her, and she shuddered at the pleasant sensation.

"How is Emma?" he wondered, his voice hoarse. There were dark marks under his eyes. His features were taut. He had suffered a restless night, like her.

She offered him a weak smile. "Better. Your family is tending to her right now. Thank you for summoning them."

He looked back toward the glass. "You needed help caring for the girl. It will be many days, if not weeks before she regains her full strength."

At least she *would* regain her strength, thought Holly . . . thanks to Quincy.

Her heart throbbed even harder. She clasped her moist hands in her lap. "You look tired."

"So do you."

"I'm going to my room to rest. I—I first wanted to make sure you were all right."

"I'm fine."

He wasn't going to offer her a confession, she realized. If she wanted to know the truth about what had possessed him in the midnight hour, she would have to ask him outright.

She took a deep breath. "What happened to you last night?"

Quincy remained silent.

She prodded, "I cried for your help, but you didn't come. I shook you, but you didn't wake."

His chest expanded as his breathing deepened, grew louder.

Holly sensed she was treading on dangerous ground, but she persisted. Something was very amiss with her husband. She wouldn't let the matter rest.

"What's wrong, Quincy? Let me help you."

The silence stretched for several more moments. He flexed his hand, then balled it into a fist. Over and over. As if fighting for control.

"It was the opium," he said at last.

She frowned. "Opium?"

"It helps me sleep."

She remembered his previous night terror, how he had cried for his mother and sister, how she had tried to rouse him without success.

"You suffer from night terrors," she concluded. "Why?"

As he had his back to her, she wasn't able to gauge his emotions, but she sensed the tension in his body.

"I killed my mother."

Holly gasped. Her heart spasmed as if a fist had rammed her in the chest. *"I'm sorry. I didn't mean to kill her"* he had cried in his disorienting sleep. But . . .

"T-that's impossible," she stuttered. "Your mother died from childbed fever."

He slumped his head. "I see you've been gossiping with Belle again."

Her spine prickled at the accusation in his voice. "Your sister isn't a gossip. She just wanted me to know . . . to understand you better."

"Then you understand I killed my mother."

"Quincy—"

"She died because I was born. Let's not mince words, Holly. I killed her."

He had the twisted idea ingrained in his soul and disabusing him of it wouldn't help matters. He'd only resist her all the more.

"Bearing a child is a risk for a woman," she agreed, "but you are not to blame for what happened to your mother."

"I am."

"Why?"

"I ruined their lives."

"They? Your family?"

"Aye." His voice dropped. "I remember the way my father looked at me, with such pain in his eyes. He'd always turn away from me, avoid me."

"Oh, Quincy."

"James assumed nursing duty, rearing us while Father was at sea. He lost his youth, keeping us in line and tending to our needs. I know how James feels toward me. Resentful. He won't admit it, but I know. And then there's Belle, a girl who grew up without a mother. And now she is a mother herself, but she doesn't always know what to do with her children. At times, I hear her cry in frustration. If our mother had lived, their lives would've been better. I should not have come into the world."

Tears rolled down her cheeks. The anguish in his voice broke her heart. "And the opium helps?"

"I can't live without it," he said in a flat vein.

"You mean . . . ?"

"I am an opium fiend, so don't be disturbed if you have trouble waking me—or if one day you cannot wake me a'tall."

Holly's heart dropped. Her world crumbled around her. She felt strapped for breath and hadn't any more words.

She grabbed her skirt and dashed from the room, rushing toward her own chamber. Inside, she slammed the door and leaned against the cool wood, sobbing.

Her heart hammered with a sense of panic she hadn't experienced in years. She suddenly remembered her father, gambling every night. She remembered the furniture disappearing from the house. She remembered rooms being shut up until only the sitting parlor remained. She remembered their meals being sparse, and the manor being cold in the winter because there wasn't fuel to heat it.

"Stop, Papa! Stop this instance!"

Her father lifted his defeated head. "I cannot stop, Holly. Not until I've restored everything that I've lost."

"If you do not stop now we will all perish."

"Holly, trust me. I will make things right."

"No," she cried. "I do not trust you anymore, Papa."

Holly staggered toward the bed and collapsed, weeping.

"No," she groaned. "Not again."

Her hope for a future with Quincy withered away. He couldn't give her what she wanted — a real marriage.

A real marriage went far beyond the marital bed, she had learned. A real marriage was structured on trust. But she could not trust her husband. Or depend on him. He was an opium fiend. He had an insatiable obsession. Just like her wastrel father. And if there was one lesson Holly had learned from her father's addiction to gambling, it was that a fiend could *never* reform his destructive ways.

CHAPTER 17

Holly parted the curtains in her sister's room, allowing light to flood the chamber. For a moment she stood in the warm glow, feeling the comforting heat on her skin, then turned from the window and smiled.

"Good morning, Emma. How do you feel?"

Emma sat up in bed. "Better."

And she was truly getting better, reflected Holly. A week had passed since her near tragic death, and with each new, hopeful day, she regained more and more of her strength.

Her heart swelling with thanksgiving, Holly took the hairbrush from the vanity and settled on the bed. Gingerly she combed her sister's tousled locks, humming a tune. The simple ritual reminded her of what she had almost lost, and she cherished the sisterly moment.

"What would you like for breakfast, dear? I can ask Cook to prepare your favorite biscuits and jam."

Emma's shoulders suddenly stiffened.

Holly pulled back the boar-bristled brush. "Is something the matter? Have I tugged too hard?"

After another tense pause, Emma said, "I would like to see Quincy."

The brush grew heavy in Holly's hand. Slowly she lowered it into her lap. "He is living aboard his brother's ship. You know that, Emma."

Quincy had moved out of the townhouse the same day he'd confessed he was an opium fiend. Holly had not asked him to leave. She had learned, after a tearful, restless sleep, that he'd packed his possessions and had advised the butler he would be aboard the *Nemesis* should anyone need him.

She still wasn't sure why he'd left. Perhaps he'd sensed her grief at his confession. Perhaps he'd wanted more privacy to indulge in his obsession. Whatever the reason for his hasty departure, he had not sent her a single message in the week he'd been away, nor had she couriered any letters to him. She just didn't know what to say to her husband anymore.

"Did he leave because of me?" asked Emma, her voice shaking. "Is he ashamed of me? H-have I ruined your marriage?"

"Oh, Emma, no." She dropped the brush and gripped her sister's shoulders. "He did not leave because of you, I promise."

If she had learned anything from her scandalous in-laws, it was that Quincy wasn't searching for perfection . . . he was searching for oblivion.

"If I did not drive him away with my . . . transgression, then why hasn't he come to visit me?"

At the sound pressure on her breast, Holly winced. "I will send word to him, invite him to visit."

"Why must you invite him? Isn't this his home?" As tears filled her confused eyes, Emma's voice finally cracked. "What have I done, Holly? Tell me. How can I make it right?"

"Stop, Emma." She embraced the girl. "Stop at once, I insist. You must conserve your energy. You *must* get well. Don't shed your strength on matters that do not concern you."

"But . . ." The girl hiccupped. "He left right after I..."

"He left because of me," said Holly.

Emma pushed her aside. "Why?"

I am an opium fiend. The chilling words still resounded in Holly's head. And what about his warning? *Don't be disturbed if you have trouble waking me – or if one day you cannot wake me a'tall.*

She shivered at the memory of his foreboding. How could she live with an opium fiend? How could she live with the constant fear he might perish in his sleep from overindulgence? How could she expose such a terrible reality to an already vulnerable Emma?

Perhaps Quincy had realized the same thing, she considered. Perhaps that was the reason he had left.

Holly bowed her head. "He is not a proper influence on you."

He wasn't dependable, like Father. He wasn't trustworthy, like Father. He wasn't safe, like Father.

"He saved my life, Holly."

"And I will be forever grateful to him, but—"

"I don't understand," she cried. "Tell me what happened? I . . . I am not a child."

Holly reared her head at the unexpected

assertion. "You most certainly are a child, and do not think otherwise. It is my duty to protect you, and I will decide what is right and proper for your ears."

Emma clamped her lips, still quivering.

But Holly held firm her position. She would not reveal the wretched truth about her husband's obsession — or her despair at losing all hope of a future with him.

As her fingers trembled, Holly scooted off the bed and returned the hairbrush to the vanity. "I will send up your breakfast."

She reached for the door latch when a broken voice whispered:

"Holly . . . ?"

That frail, frightened voice disarmed her, and she whirled around.

"Oh, Emma, I'm sorry I was so cross with you." Bustling toward the bed, Holly hugged her sibling, then smoothed the girl's tresses away from her tear-soaked cheeks. "I am not myself."

Her sister managed a crooked smile. "We make an unhappy pair, don't we?"

"Yes, most unhappy." Tears also pooled in Holly's eyes. "I had hoped things would be different. After losing Mama and Papa . . . Well, we mustn't dwell on the past."

"And the future?"

"I'm afraid I don't know what the future holds, my dear."

She hoped the Hawkins family would remain kind to her and Emma, despite the estrangement between Holly and their brother. If not, there was still the cottage on the outskirts of London. She and

Emma could always retire there, especially if word ever spread of her sister's "transgression."

Emma nodded. "We have each other."

"Yes, we do." She smiled. "And we will *always* have each other." A pause, then, "Emma, I must know the truth. Who hurt you?"

Since the girl had regained much of her strength, Holly felt it time to broach the uncomfortable matter—though she waited with baited breath to hear the villain's identity.

"You must tell me, Emma."

"I know." She averted her eyes. "What will happen to him?"

At the obvious concern in her sister's voice, Holly's hackles spiked. The cur had seduced an innocent maiden and she *worried* for him? His wicked trickery had beguiled the poor dear, indeed.

"Do not trouble yourself with that, Emma. Tell me his name."

After a few thoughtful moments, she heaved a breath. "Bobbie."

Bobbie? Bobbie? Holly searched her memory. When had she encountered a Bobbie?

"Wait," said Holly. "Bobbie? As in Robert? Our old farm boy?"

Again Emma nodded.

Holly lifted to her feet, her mind a whirl. "I-I don't understand. Is Robert in Town?"

"No," said Emma, curling her arms around her raised knees. "I—we were together the night before you and I moved to London."

Holly dropped her head and groaned.

"A-are you angry, Holly?"

Aye, she was angry. Angry at herself. She had failed to recognize an attachment had formed between Emma and Robert. The farm lad had worked at the cottage for many years. He was Emma's age. And the girl had so few friends, isolated in the country as she was. Of course she'd developed a bond with the boy. Holly should have paid closer attention to the two, but she had considered them children, innocent of the greater world and its earthly desires. She couldn't even rally her rage against Robert, a mere boy.

Holly plopped back on the bed and sighed. "I am not angry, dear. I should have warned you . . . talked to you about matters of love and marriage."

Emma's cheeks glowed bright. "I'm sorry, Holly."

"It's all right, love."

"What will happen to Bobbie?"

"I don't know."

What to do? thought Holly. Should she contact Robert's father and demand his son marry Emma? What about Emma's future in London? Her opportunity to meet and marry a gentleman?

"Do you still care for Robert?"

Emma lowered her lashes. "I love him."

"Why didn't you tell me?"

"I didn't think you would approve."

"Well, I suppose I would not have approved. You are a viscount's daughter. You deserve to marry a gentleman."

"I'm not too fond of the gentlemen in society. I was excited to meet them at first. But . . . They are not like Bobbie."

"And what is 'Bobbie' like?"

"He makes me laugh. He teaches me about the land. He looks at me like I'm a princess." Her voice dropped. "I miss him."

Holly sighed again. She considered forbidding the couple from ever seeing one another again, but since her own marriage had unfolded so poorly, the rigid restriction seemed unjust.

"I will make you a compromise, Emma."

The girl lifted her anxious eyes.

"In two years time, *if* you and Robert are still in love, I will not prevent your courtship."

Emma opened her mouth.

"*But*," stressed Holly, "you must make every effort to meet the gentlemen in society, to truly learn and know the desires of your heart. I want you to be happy, Emma."

The girl simpered. "Thank you, Holly."

She released yet another disgruntled sigh. "And why didn't you tell me you were pregnant, Emma?"

"I thought you would disown me . . . like you disowned Papa."

"What? I—I never disowned Papa."

"I heard you in the study, Holly. The night before he died."

Holly remembered that terrible night, and her heart pounded . . .

"Stop, Papa! Stop this instance!"

Her father lifted his defeated head. "I cannot stop, Holly. Not until I've restored everything that I've lost."

"If you do not stop now we will all perish."

"Holly, trust me. I will make things right."

"No," she cried. "I do not trust you anymore, Papa."

"Holly —"

"If you do not stop now, then you are not my Papa!"

A knot formed in Holly's throat, making it hard to breathe. Had she really disowned her father with those last words? She was angry with him, true. But...

Holly tasted the salty tears as they stained her cheeks and lips. She remembered the look in her father's eyes when he'd heard she'd lost her faith in him. Hope had died. And he had died soon after, placing a pistol to his head.

A sob ripped from the bowel of her belly. "Oh, my God!"

"What is it, Holly? What's the matter?'

"I—I killed Papa."

Emma paled. "You. Shot. Him?"

"No!" She gasped. "I broke his heart, and he . . . and he died because of me."

Overwhelmed by crippling spasms of guilt, Holly bolted from the room. She charged into her bedchamber and secured the door. Alone inside, she paced the floor, her palms covering her trembling mouth.

What had she done? She had pushed her father, already a broken man, into deeper despair. She had taken away his hope.

Holly, trust me. I will make things right.

But she had not trusted him. Not anymore. She had *denied* him.

You are not my Papa!

He was gone the next morning.

Holly collapsed on the bed, sobbing.

CHAPTER 18

Quincy sat on the bed, staring at the opium capsules in his hand. Something pressed on his mind, urging him to swallow the entire batch.

Since moving aboard the *Nemesis*, he had grown wearier. He desired rest. Real rest. After two years of near constant battle, he was tired of fighting the shadows he now knew would never leave him in peace.

He shut his eyes, evoking the memory of a warm, white light—and Holly. He remembered the vision he'd had a week ago, when he'd stopped breathing, of fiery tresses spilling over him, pierced by brilliant light, of leaf green eyes shining with warmth, of a smile—a smile that chased away every shadow.

Slowly he opened his eyes. In the dark cabin, he yearned to return to that moment. He would only ever find it in sleep. He knew he would never share real intimacy with Holly, not after she'd learned he was an opium fiend.

Quincy had tried to hide the truth from her, from himself. But there wasn't any sense in denying it after the night his sister-in-law had almost died. It had been clear to his wife then that something was the matter with him. And like his brothers, she was disgusted by his obsession.

He had heard her sorrowful tears when he'd approached her bedroom door later that same day. And without another thought, he'd left the townhouse. She didn't want him anymore. And that truth, that wretched truth, twisted his innards with a pain that took his breath away.

"You wanted her indifference, fool," he abased himself. "And you have it."

The capsules in his palm grew heavy. His hand trembled. He hadn't taken opium in days, allowing the night terrors to torture him. But his muscles now cramped in hunger for the drug. And he had no reason to resist their ravenous demand.

The cabin door opened.

"Get out," he snarled without averting his eyes from the opium. There were a handful of tars aboard ship, guarding the vessel while she was anchored in port.

"But, sir?"

"Out!" he stormed.

"That's all right, Thomas," said a feminine voice. "Thank you for escorting me."

Quincy reared his head as Holly entered the cabin carrying a lamp and carpetbag She set down her luggage and closed the door, turning the key in the lock. To his greater astonishment, she then removed the key and wedged it between her breasts, imprisoning him.

"It's much too dark in here," she groused and bustled around the room, lighting the other lamps.

143

"There."

The room aglow, she pivoted and spotted the pile of capsules in his palm. Her eyes widened. "*What* are you doing?"

She smacked his hand, scattering the drug, and crushed the opium beneath her heels.

"Were you going to take those?" She pointed at the floor. "All of those?"

She slapped him across the face.

"Blimey!" he roared, finally finding his voice. "What the devil was that for?"

"For even thinking of leaving me!"

He sucked in a desperate breath, his mind buzzing with myriad thoughts. What was she doing here? Had something happened at home?

"What's the matter?" he demanded.

"I beg your pardon?"

"Is it Emma? Is she all right?"

Holly sighed. "Emma is fine. She is under your sister's care."

As he massaged his smarting cheek, Quincy narrowed his eyes on the woman. He couldn't fathom the reason for her being aboard ship. Or for her outburst. As if she . . .

His heart jerked at the thought that she cared for him, and he squelched the fanciful idea before it took root in his already battered soul.

"Then why are you here?" he asked, voice taut, muscles even tauter.

"I can't visit my husband?"

"Do not lie to me, Holly." He glanced at her carpetbag. Why would she come to "visit" him in the dead of night? "What's wrong?"

Holly stepped toward the porthole and peered through the glass. "I came to tell you I understand how you feel."

Quincy looked away from her. He rubbed his hands together, mulling over her inexplicable remark. Soon he heard her loud, rasping breaths. Was she weeping?

He glanced at her askance. Her shoulders quivered. Something had obviously grieved her. But why had she come to him? For comfort? He usually sensed a woman's desire without trouble, but this time . . .

"Why are you here?" he wondered once more.

"To keep you safe," she whispered.

His heart pounded again, and that damn fanciful longing struggled to root itself in his soul. "Do I need safe keeping?"

"Yes," she said without hesitation. "You are a danger to yourself, Quincy. And it's my duty to protect you."

"Your duty?"

"I made a vow." She wiped her tears and confronted him, her eyes still glassy. "For better for worse, for richer for poorer, in sickness and in health. And I intend to keep my word."

Her demeanor had changed. She carried something heavy upon her shoulders. And whatever it was, it had turned her world upside-down. That much he sensed without misgiving.

"You and I do not have a real marriage, Holly. I wed you to save your reputation."

"I know," she returned softly.

"Then *why* are you here?"

"I've decided not to give up on you."

His thoughts churned in even greater confusion. Why did she give him a different answer each time he asked her the same simple question: why are you here? Was it possible all three answers were true?

Holly treaded across the room and grabbed her carpetbag. She carried it over to the desk and unpacked a few of her belongings.

"You had best get comfortable," she said. "You and I are going to stay in this cabin for a long while."

Slowly he stood, his muscles still aching for opium, his body breaking into a cold sweat. "And if I want out of this room?"

"You won't search for the key. We both know you vowed never to touch me."

"I vowed never to bed you."

She waved a dismissive hand. "That's neither here nor there."

Quincy headed for the door.

She dashed toward it, too, barricading it with her body. "If you want out of this cabin, you'll have to go through me."

The steely look in her eyes told him she was adamant.

He curled his fingers into fists. He need only shove her aside and kick down the wood. He had the strength to do it . . . but the thought of putting his hands on her in any rough manner made him ill.

He backed away from her, his heart hammering. "I can't stay here forever."

"I should hope not."

"Damn it, I can't live without—"

"Opium, yes, I remember. Well, I also know the

opiates don't help you anymore since you continue to have night terrors." She stepped away from the door and approached him. "You cannot resist the temptation of opium, I understand, so *I* will keep the temptation from you."

Take away the temptation of opium and replace it with the temptation of *her*?

"You're mad," he said bluntly.

She squared her shoulders, affronted. "I want to help you, Quincy."

"Then leave me be, wench."

"No."

Her decisive "no" stabbed deeper than a knife.

He was trapped.

CHAPTER 19

W hen Holly opened her tired eyes, she was alone in the bed. Scanning the cabin in the morning light, she quickly realized she was also alone in the room.

"Bloody hell." She scrambled to her feet and groped between her breasts, searching for the key. "That pirate!"

Holly rushed from the room. For two weeks she'd nursed the blackguard through the pangs of insatiable cravings, bouts of irritability, cold then hot sweats, retchings and tremors—and he dared to escape *now*.

She'd wring his miserable neck, she would. She had suffered right alongside him, every dreadful moment. And on more than one occasion, she'd even feared he might truly perish during a convulsion, that perhaps he really couldn't live without opium. But each attack on his body had lessened in severity with time, and soon there were fewer and fewer attacks.

For much of his confinement, Quincy hadn't even

noticed her presence. If he wasn't in a dead sleep, he was groaning in agony. She would often curl up beside him on the bed, when he'd collapsed in fatigue, her own bones aching for rest.

Holly scaled the hatch in her bare feet and stepped onto the deck. How could he sneak away in such a cowardly manner after all she'd done for—?

Her tirade of thoughts came to an abrupt end when she noticed her husband standing at the stern of the ship, gazing out at the Thames.

Her cheeks warmed as she recalled her scathing rebukes of him, and after a few measured breaths, she calmed her raging heart.

Approaching his tall figure, she settled beside him.

"I needed air," he said in a flat vein, clearly guessing her thoughts. He handed her the cabin key. "I didn't want to wake you."

She took the key from him, rubbing the metal between her fingers. "How do you feel?"

"Like shit."

Quincy turned his deep blue eyes toward her, and though they were bloodshot, and his voice was hoarse and surly, she knew he would be all right, really all right, because for the first time in two weeks he *saw* her.

"You look tired," he murmured.

A light wind ruffled her already tousled hair, and she brushed the stray tresses behind her ear. "I look like a fright."

"No." He thumbed her check. "You look like a siren from the sea."

She shuddered under his gentle caress and heady

149

words, her skin tingling with gooseflesh. She had longed for his tender touch, his intimate endearments, and she closed her eyes, pressing her cheek into his warm palm, sighing with pleasure as he stroked her jaw . . . her lips.

Her breath hitched. He thumbed her mouth in light yet sensual sweeps, and her heart pounded again.

Her lashes fluttered. She met his smoldering stare. He reached for her. She parted her lips . . . but he pulled her into his arms.

Holly sighed again. Not in disappointment, though. The man's strong embrace comforted her as much as his healing kiss, and she clinched his waist in return, laying her cheek over his strapping chest. At the sound of his thundering heart, her relief intensified.

I didn't lose you.

A sob welled in her throat, the anxiety she'd suppressed for the last two weeks now bursting in her breast. She hugged him even harder, and he smothered the crown of her head with his mouth, soothing her in a hushed tone.

"How can you heal others, but not yourself?" she wondered when her nerves stilled and her fears faded away.

"I don't know." A pause, then, "I still have night terrors."

"And you'll have to face them without the opium."

"How is that better?"

She looked up at him, connected with his troubled gaze. "Because now you'll face them with me at your side."

His uneasy expression softened. "With you?"

"Aye."

Grazing her spine with his fingertips, he rubbed the length of her backside over and over until her blood swelled with want and heat.

"Why don't you go below and rest?" he whispered in a throaty voice.

"I don't want to leave your side. I'm so thankful I didn't lose you, too."

"Too?" His eyes widened. "Emma . . . ?"

"Emma is fine," she swiftly assured him. "Mirabelle sends word of her progress every day. She's already up and about, taking strolls through the garden." She hesitated. "I meant my father."

The pain she'd smothered while nursing her husband now slammed against her ribs, taking her breath away. She still heard her father's plaintive voice in her mind: *Holly, trust me. I will make things right.* And she still heard her cold rebuff: *No, I do not trust you anymore, Papa.*

She trembled at the memory and tears filled her eyes.

Quincy wiped the drops from her cheeks, smearing the briny moisture. "What happened to your family?"

She turned her head and observed the fiery sunrise reflecting across the Thames. "I had a happy childhood. Mama and Papa were always joyful, full of life. They hosted parties almost every week." She smiled in nostalgia, but her lips soon slipped, and her frown returned. "Papa, like every other lord, enjoyed a good card game, winning a few hands, losing others. But his pastime turned obsessive when he lost too many hands in a row. He was determined to regain every shilling. He couldn't, though. With each attempt, he lost more. And more. He grew desperate." She sucked in a frantic breath. "He wouldn't stop."

The set of arms around her tightened, squeezing the panic from her heart.

"He lost everything, I assume," said Quincy.

She nodded. "Even his life."

"His life?"

Her throat constricted as she resumed the tale. "He took his life with a pistol."

"I'm sorry, Holly."

"I am even sorrier." Her watery eyes lifted. "We argued the night before his suicide. I pleaded with him to stop gambling. He pleaded with me to trust him, that he would restore all that he'd taken from us." Her voice ragged, she stuttered, "I-I didn't trust him anymore, though. And I turned away from him. He died the next day. Because of me."

He furrowed his brow. "How is it your fault?"

Her tears fell quick. "When I lost faith in Papa, I took away his hope. He had no reason to live after that."

Holly sensed the moment her husband's posture toward her changed, shifted with an uncertain tightness.

"Is that why you came to me?" he asked, voice guarded.

"I came to help you."

He stepped back, releasing her, and that familiar panic surged in her breast, the same panic she'd battled as a young woman, when she'd realized her father had squandered the family's fortune.

"What's wrong, Quincy?"

"I just thought . . . No, it doesn't matter."

"Of course it matters. Tell me."

An unexpected melancholy entered his beautiful eyes. "I thought you'd come aboard ship because you cared for me."

There was a rawness in his voice that smacked of hurt, starling her. "I *do* care for you. How can you think otherwise?"

"No, you care about your guilt. You came aboard the *Nemesis* looking for absolution. But I am not your father, Holly."

Her thoughts reeled. Her blood raced. Wavering, she reached for the ship's rail. "I don't understand."

"Let it be, Holly."

He turned and sauntered away.

"Wait!" she cried, feeling dizzy, strapped for breath. "Where are you going?"

"I'm going home."

"What's happened, Quincy?" Her lungs ached for air. "Why are you walking away? I—I love you!"

He hardened in his tracks.

She heaved under the incredible weight of those words. As she stood there, alone, watching her husband leave, imagining a life without him, the load intensified, and a fierce need possessed her.

"You are my husband. And I love you, Quincy Hawkins." She moved away from the rail and circled him, glaring right into his confused eyes. "Don't you dare push me away with that infernal excuse. I'm not here looking for absolution. I'm here because I love you, and I don't want to lose you."

"Like you lost your father?"

"Yes! Yes, like I lost my father. I should have helped him all those years ago. But I didn't. And that is *my* pain. But I can help *you*. I can be here for *you*."

He raked an unsteady hand through his hair, still perturbed, unbelieving.

"Why are you so afraid of me?" she demanded.

He reared his head. "What?"

"Trust me. Touch me. *Be* with me." Her voice faltered. "We can be happy together, I know it."

At the turmoil still swirling in his eyes, she knew she hadn't convinced him of the truth—and that sparked a flash of anger in her.

"Fine," she snapped. "Be alone. I will still love you, you damn pirate."

And she stalked away.

CHAPTER 20

Slumped in an armchair, a glass of brandy in his hand, Quincy stared at the unfinished self-portrait of Holly. He'd wandered into her art studio, unable to sleep, and had found the charcoal sketch still perched on the easel. And still mesmerizing.

A burst of lightning filled the room, followed by roaring thunder. He rubbed his burning eyes and turned away from his wife's haunting likeness, downing the remaining brandy.

When he'd arrived home earlier that day, a cheerful Emma had received him, followed by a proud Mirabelle, and for the first time in a long time, he'd felt grateful to be alive, that he had been there to help the girl.

His wife had not been there to welcome him, though. According to his sister, Holly had returned to the house, escorted by one of his shipmates, and after greeting her kin, had gone straight to her room where she was still secured. His sister had left thereafter, sensing the discord between the newlyweds. But Quincy had not approached his wife's room. It was after midnight, and he still had not neared her chamber door. In truth, he also felt like a canon ball had rammed him in the gut.

He pushed out of the armchair. Surrounded by shrouded canvases, he had an overwhelming urge to unmask them and stripped away the drapings, revealing painting after brilliant painting. Still, the need to unveil his wife consumed him. He ransacked her paper sketches, sifting through portraits and stills and abstract designs. Her talent was boundless, undeniable, but his need to expose her went unsatisfied. He'd already recognized her scope as an artist. What was he really searching for?

Proof.

He slumped his shoulders at the dismal revelation. He was searching for proof that she loved him. He hadn't found it, though. There were no moonstruck images of him amongst the piles of papers, no dewy-eyed oils. The one nude she'd produced of him had been for profit, and not a sentiment of her true affection for him.

There was nothing in the studio to support her declaration of love.

"Damn it."

He leaned against the wall and closed his eyes. Fear filled him. A fear of what, though? And how had that fear just sprouted in his breast?

Quincy stalked toward the door—then stilled. At a certain angle, the charcoal portrait of Holly stared straight at him. Before, it'd appeared as if she was looking sidelong to some distant, unnamed point, but standing where he was now, he met her eyes dead-on.

His heart capered, and that unnamed fear revealed itself: what if she didn't truly love him?

What if she was using him to make peace with her past? What if he was just a substitute for her father, a means of reparation and reconciliation? Once, such a thought would not have troubled him. But now . . .

Quincy inhaled a desperate breath. As he gazed into her sooty eyes, filled with myriad emotions, he longed for her love because . . . because he loved her.

He shuddered under the force of those words; they permeated his soul until he pulsed with an insatiable desire for Holly. But that fear still gripped him. What if her professed love for him wasn't real? He couldn't imagine a greater hell than to be in love with his wife and not have her love in return. Or what if she rejected him after their morning quarrel? What if he was too late, and she'd hardened her heart against him?

Quincy steadied his irregular breathing. He couldn't remember a more critical battle than the one raging in his heart right now. And he realized there was no winning the battle by scouring the art studio or torturing himself with endless questions of doubt. There was really only one thing he could do — surrender to his love for Holly, consequences be damned.

Holly wrapped her arms around her bare shoulders, a light breeze in the humid air. She stood on the balcony in her night rail, watching the moon-washed garden below. Soon the celestial light faded as storm clouds encroached. She listened to the angry thunder still miles off and travelled away in her thoughts, escaping the dull ache in her breast.

Her husband's accusation still rattled in her head: *you care about your guilt . . . absolution . . . I am not your father*. No, he was not. And she wasn't striving to change the past. Her father was dead, and she was left with two disjointed sentiments: asking his forgiveness for her weakness and forgiving him for his. She'd not known about the power of hope or encouragement, that a lost soul could be guided home with a loving hand. But she understood the lesson now. And she'd *no* regrets helping her husband. Her only regret was growing attached to the man.

Quincy had told her time and again he wanted a marriage in name alone. She should have believed him. She should have helped him overcome his obsession without wishing for more.

She was a fool for dreaming. And now she was a fool in love.

"Damn."

The sting of bitter tears blurred her vision, and she wiped away the annoying droplets, vowing never to weep over the pirate again.

A gentle rain fell, a mist really, and she closed her eyes, allowing the spray to bathe her, perhaps wash away her sorrow.

Holly tensed.

A draft stirred at her backside. Her languid heart jumped. And a shiver skittered along her spine.

She grabbed the iron rail for support. She was confused. And ravenous. Fearful. And hoping. Always foolishly hoping.

He stepped through the balcony doors, silent, and

the fine hairs on her arms spiked. She flexed her fingers, then grasped the rail again. Tight. So tight. She waited for him to speak, but he remained still — earth-shatteringly still.

The longer he stood behind her, his primal gaze burrowing into her, the more her senses roared with life. But she would not confront him. He had come to her. In the dead of night. Why?

"W-why are you here?" she stammered.

Quincy took another step toward her.

Her breath hitched.

"I saw the light under your door," he murmured.

"That's not an answer." In a strangled voice, she asked again, "Why are you here?"

She strengthened her hold on the rail, her knees weakening. The rain now poured. And the pressure in her chest ballooned until she was sure her heart might fail her. She had never waited with such anticipation, such dread, such miserable hope. She almost whirled around and smacked him for making her stand there in agony.

Again, he moved toward her with heady intent. Oh, heavens! She couldn't feel her fingers anymore, she was holding the iron barrier so hard. Her heart pounded in her ears. She trembled. Her lungs throbbed for air. A powerful yearning coursed through her veins.

Please, don't be a dream.

When his hips brushed hers, she gasped. An almost electric shock passed through her. In the storm, she might've believed lightning had pierced her soul, but she knew it wasn't the turbulent sky that'd ravaged her — it was her husband.

159

Holly remained taut as he nestled more firmly against her backside. At last she relaxed into him, consuming the strength, the warmth, the intimacy he offered her in that moment. But he had not confessed his intentions. Aye, his body whispered his sensual desires, but his lips had yet to reveal the true workings of his heart. Had he come for a mere tussle? Or had he come searching for something more?

His broad hands slipped between their heated bodies and he unraveled the stays of his shirt, pulling the garment over his head and tossing it to the ground.

She took in a ragged breath. "What are you doing?"

And if he stated the obvious, she *would* turn around and clout him.

He next unfastened the flaps of his trousers, the subtle movements whisking across her lower spine, making her quiver.

"I'm giving you my body."

Her heart seized. In a near inaudible voice, she whispered, "Why?"

He curled his naked form around her, and she opened her mouth in silent ecstasy, unable to utter a sound. His every muscle throbbed with indisputable want—for her—and she raked her teeth over her bottom lip, resisting complete surrender. She just had to know . . .

"Why?" she demanded, still waiting to hear words that might mend—or further tear—her heart.

His fingers trailed up her rigid arms, slick with rain and peppered with gooseflesh. He caressed her shoulders, pressed his thumbs deep into her shoulder blades, forcing her to arch backward. At the unexpected pleasure of his manipulating touch, she cried out.

He then dropped his wet brow and rested it on the crown of her head, his rough voice rumbling, "Because I love you."

A sob of joy welled in her throat. Hope sprouted anew. Still, she was unsure about his admission. "I thought you didn't want — ?"

"I was wrong," he said hoarsely. "I want you, Holly. I want you more than I've ever wanted anything in my life."

As tremors pulsed through his hands, vibrating down her arms, she sensed his misgiving. After all they had been through, would she accept his love?

Tears filled her eyes again. She appreciated all the more his sincerity, his bravery in the face of uncertain rejection.

He belonged to her, she accepted in that moment. Truly, he belonged to her. And she belonged to him. Forever. And not because of a scandalous painting or a forced marriage, but because he loved her, as she loved him.

"Sweet Holly," he seduced in a hushed tone. "Be my wife."

And she sighed between falling tears to *finally* hear him call her "sweet" again. "I should wallop you but good for taking so long to give in."

A chuckle resounded in his chest, making her smile, too. "I will spend the rest of my life making it up to you, I promise."

The energy between them changed, shifted from

wavering doubt and hope to cardinal desire. Without hesitation, he hooked the straps of her night rail around his thumbs, dragging them off her shoulders. "Starting tonight," he breathed into her ear. "Our wedding night."

Our wedding night.

She shut her eyes at the cherished, long sought after words. An anxious want filled her belly and spread throughout her essence as her breathing grew swift and shallow.

Since her garment clinched her body like a second skin, he peeled away the soaked linen until it dropped to the ground, leaving her naked in the stormy night. Water pelted her skin. She shivered under the stimulating taction.

"You're so beautiful," he rasped.

Her blood swelled. Her lips, her breasts felt fuller, more sensitive. She wasn't even abashed at the admiration in his gruff voice; it offered her nothing but delight.

"You're beautiful, too," she returned softly, perhaps a little wickedly. "I've already had the pleasure of seeing you in the buff."

He grunted at her impudence. "Wench."

But her grin faltered when he brushed aside her damp hair and nuzzled the crook between her neck and shoulder, bussing the tender flesh while circling her waist . . . and kneading her breasts.

Holly moaned. Her heart rammed against her breastbone in arousal, such wanton arousal. She had never experienced more rapture or beauty. As her husband stroked her aching nipples, sucked at her supple throat, undulated at her bare back, she nigh dropped from the assailing sensations.

"Hold the rail, Holly. Tight."

A violent shudder wracked her limbs. She obeyed, squeezing the iron bar. His knuckles traced the knobs of her spine. Water sluiced her body. And then his robust fingers slipped between her buttocks.

She arced on pointe at the man's probing thrusts, at the intense titillation. An exquisite tension gathered between her thighs, and her quim—oh, heavens—her quim wetted with fierce need.

In instinct, she spread her legs apart, wanting more.

So much more.

With a feral longing that matched her own, Quincy grabbed her hips, pulled her arse closer toward him, and penetrated her core in one hot, hard stroke.

Sweet heavens!

CHAPTER 21

Quincy dropped his head back and groaned. His wife's tight, wet quim gripped him with insatiable need. He'd never experienced such profound pleasure. As the rain battered him and her carnal cries filled his ears, he surrendered to the madness: the sweet, sweet madness.

He thrust into her, again and again, flexing his muscles, maintaining control of his depth and rhythm so as not to cause her too much pain. Soon her body softened with every sensual undulation. And her unbound passion disarmed him. As always.

Whatever had possessed him to resist her? Whatever had possessed him to think he *could* resist her? From the moment he'd met her at the gaming hell, from the moment he'd kissed her in his carriage, he'd known — intuitively — he belonged to her.

And she belonged to him.

Holly opened for him without resistance. She opened every part of herself. Her heart. Her soul. Her womb. She took his breath away. And he anchored her hips in a firm hold, rocking her faster and faster.

As her cries strengthened, as her quim clenched and pulsed, he sensed her approaching climax and quickened his penetration, pumping her even harder.

His heart raged. His hips bucked. And then she shouted in pure ecstasy, her muscles throbbing around his erection. She came so fast. Her warm fluids streaked his thighs. And he blessedly released his own orgasm, pouring his seed into her, grinding her arse in one final, desperate stroke of lust.

Quincy captured the iron rail, gasping for breath. He buried his brow in Holly's tangled hair and covered her with his fevered flesh.

Soon she turned in his embrace, her eyes smoldering, her lips flushed with blood. "Kiss me," she whispered, ransacking his soul with the impassioned entreaty. "Kiss me as your wife."

Another groan. He gathered her in his shaking arms. Skin nestled skin. Not even raindrops slipped between them. So close. That's how he wanted her. Always.

Quincy took her mouth in a gentle kiss, lingering over one swollen lip then the other. Again, one lip then the other. And again. He tasted her. Explored her. He sensed her every want—softness, intimacy, affection—and offered it all without hesitancy. The kiss stripped him raw. She rent every last vestige of darkness from his soul and inserted herself in its place. Christ, he almost broke under the breadth of her love.

Deeper, he kissed her. Ached for her. Every part of her. And she matched his growing arousal, burrowing her fingers into his neck, tenderness giving way to fire.

"Oh, Holly," he murmured, reaching for the curvature at her throat. "Sweet Holly."

There, he rested his lips. Her pulse thundered beneath his tongue, and he bussed and nipped at the supple flesh, ravenous. He laved her shoulder, stroked her collar bone, then caressed the hollow between her breasts.

Discovering his wife's body was like exploring an uncharted part of himself, and with each new, sensuous find he took in more of her and revealed more of himself in return.

She trembled under his ministrations, evoking his primal instincts. He dropped to his knees, rubbing her shapely hips, bussing her taut abdomen . . . her moist thighs.

Holly clamped her hands over the iron rail and arched her back. She offered him a divine position to thoroughly probe and taste and know her.

And he accepted her beautiful offer.

"Lift your leg," he bade in a desperate vein.

Slowly she hoisted a quivering limb, hooking it over his shoulder.

His blood flowed hot at the swirl of auburn curls shielding her quim. He parted the hair with his thumb, exposing her sultry flesh, and a savage hunger quickly ravaged his belly.

He cupped her moist quim in his mouth, moaning in carnal gratification. As he sucked her sensitive skin, she wetted in his mouth. He moaned louder, stronger. He thrust his salacious tongue into her dewy folds. Her muscles constricted. He plunged even deeper. Ravished her. Over and over.

"Come, sweet," he begged, hoarse. "Come."

And when she orgasmed in his mouth, Quincy shuddered in violent satisfaction. His pulse pounded between his ears with such force, he hardly heard the storm. But he heard Holly's sobs. Her sobs of pleasure.

"Come to bed," she enticed in a throaty whisper.

He looked up at her, still struggling for breath, but there was no mistaking the inferno in her eyes. She grabbed his hand, guiding him into the bedroom, and together they tumbled onto the feather mattress.

Quickly he found himself tangled in her arms and legs and hair. "Holly, are you sure? I don't want to hurt you."

He had broken her maidenhead, and he wasn't certain she could endure another coupling so soon, but when she scraped her fingernails roughly down his back and pumped his arse, he growled, blood burning. "Blimey."

"Trust me," she beseeched. "Touch me. *Be* with me," she implored, mirroring her petition earlier in the day.

And he groaned in abject surrender . . . though he vowed to love her ever so slow.

Quincy opened his eyes as morning light entered the room and spread across the bed. The white light formed a fine line over a woman's slumbering profile. It caressed her throat and travelled down her chest and across the peaks of her naked breasts.

She stirred under the warm light, turned her head away from it. Her lashes fluttered, her dreamy green eyes appeared—and she smiled.

His chest ached under the spell of her brilliant smile, more brilliant than the white light. A hand reached for him and stroked his temple, his cheek, and he sighed at the soothing touch. But when a finger traced the contours of his mouth, a simmering heat stirred in his belly.

"Good morning," she whispered.

He was strapped for breath, for words. Holly rolled over him, her red hair spilling around him, sheltering him. Her smile never weakened. She brushed his chin with her thumb before her mouth covered his in a sensual kiss.

When he opened his eyes again, her beautiful smile remained. Beams of light pierced her hair and flashed across her brow and nose. He wrapped his arms around her back, holding her tight.

"Am I dreaming?" he wondered, his mind cloudy with a sense of familiarity.

"I hope not." She bussed him again. "But if you are, don't wake up. Don't ever wake up."

He dragged in a draft of air as he remembered his dream—and the night he had almost perished from opium. That he might have missed this prophetic moment—and every future, loving moment—with Holly twisted his heart.

Her brow creased. "Is anything the matter?"

He cupped her warm cheek and pulled her down for another tender kiss. "Not a damn thing, wife."

EPILOGUE

Q uincy gazed around the sitting room, a drink in his hand. It was the eve before his brother's wedding, and the entire family had gathered for a late night supper at Holly's behest. She was being very secretive about the impromptu festivities. There was a draped canvas in the corner of the room that drew Quincy's wary eye. His wife had cuffed him more than once for trying to catch a glimpse of the artwork before the official unveiling. Though he trusted it wasn't another nude, her furtive behavior unsettled him just a bit.

Forcing himself to avoid the mysterious painting, Quincy noticed his brother, William, also regarding the family from afar. He wasn't engaged in the spirited chatter, though his expression remained thoughtful, even peaceful. The uncharacteristic melancholy that'd overshadowed him had lifted, indicating his troubles had been resolved. At least, Quincy hoped it the case. His enigmatic, impassive elder brother was always the most difficult to read.

A cheerful Emma bounded toward him next, her cheeks a rosy pink. He thanked the Lord each time she greeted him with that beaming smile. And he shuddered at the memory of her near demise, his own intoxication on the night she and his wife had so desperately needed him. If he'd failed to treat the girl, or worse, if he'd made a mistake to hasten her death, he would never have forgiven himself. Guilt was a heavy, at times intolerable, burden, he knew.

"What do you think it is?" she asked, pointing toward the veiled painting, the infernal painting that was starting to gnaw on his nerves.

"I've no idea," he grumbled.

"She's worked on it night and day, every day. I've not seen her in weeks!"

"Nor I," he grumbled again, thinking of the quiet nights he'd spent pacing their bedroom, restless and unable to sleep without Holly in his arms. On several lonely occasions, he'd even found himself outside her studio door, listening to her creative movements within. And on more than one occasion, he'd considered breaking down the barrier and dragging her away from her obsessive work. He'd worried about her health. He'd worried about her mind. He'd worried about *her*. About being apart from her. On their bloody honeymoon.

But Holly's talents would not be suppressed. At year's end, she would formally show a collection of her work at an art gallery. Quincy had paid for the rental and publicity. His wife would sign each piece with the enigmatic initials H. H. and allow the public to view her work without any preconceived notions about her gender or station in life. The critics would have to look at her work—and her work alone—and form their judgments based solely on her talent.

As vibrant laughter filled the room, Quincy turned his head and caught sight of his wife's dazzling smile. In an instant, his chest tightened. His thoughts shifted. And a healing warmth spread throughout his body, seeping into his bones.

He marveled at her brilliant smile: at its ability to chase away dark reflections and set the world right in his heart. She cocked her head and winked at him, having sensed his heated gaze, knowing he wanted her at his side. From the start of their marriage, she'd had that uncanny knack.

After a few more merry words with his kin, Holly excused herself and sauntered toward him with a fire in her eyes that matched his own.

"*When* will you unveil the painting?" demanded Emma. "It's almost midnight."

"Soon, my dear," she assured her sister. "I just need a word with my husband."

Emma sighed and walked off.

As his wife's smoldering expression fixed on him again, his pulse quickened, and he had the urge to express the very same demand: *When will you unveil the painting? It's almost midnight . . . And I want you in our bed.*

"Well?" he drawled.

She lifted a teasing brow. "Well what?"

"You know damn well 'well what'."

She chuckled, a sensual sound. "I'll show you mine when you show me yours."

"I beg your pardon?"

"The letter. I know it arrived today. If you want to see the painting, show me the letter."

His muscles relaxed. And then he frowned at his

shifty wife. How had she known about the letter? Was she spying on him? The servants, he thought. She'd probably ordered them to mole about on her behalf.

"Well?" she drawled this time.

Quincy pulled the sealed missive from his inner coat pocket, handing it to Holly.

"You haven't opened it yet?"

He shook his head. "I was waiting until after the wedding."

"But why?"

He shrugged. "I didn't want the disappointing news to distract me during the nuptials. I have to be there for Eddie and Amy."

"I have faith in you," she said softly, her voice rich with confidence. "Don't assume the news will be disappointing . . . Can I open it?"

After taking a fortifying breath, he nodded in assent.

Holly carefully broke the wax seal and unfurled the papers. She scanned the lines, her expression blank.

"And?" he demanded after several silent moments had passed.

She folded the letter. "And what?"

"What does it say, wench?"

She returned coyly, "I thought you didn't want to know until after the wedding? . . . Doctor Quincy Hawkins."

He delved into her shining eyes, searching for clarity. "Truly?"

She offered him the papers.

Skimming the flourished penmanship, Quincy

read the announcement of his accreditation with the Royal College of Physicians.

"Congratulations," she whispered.

He pocketed the letter, rather bemused. "Thank you."

Holly wrapped her arms around his waist, squeezing him tight. He returned her joyful embrace, still in disbelief. The idea, nay the desire, to work formally in medicine had been stirring in his heart for some time. It was only after his sister-in-law's near death he'd realized just how much he'd wanted to improve his knowledge, his skill and work in a hospital or perhaps even open a private practice. It would mean leaving his post aboard the *Nemesis*, though. He would have to tell his brother soon, after the wedding.

Doctor Quincy Hawkins, he mused. *That* would take getting used to.

"I've shown you mine," he murmured into her ear. "Now show me yours."

She looked up at him, her cheeks flushed with color. "If you insist."

Holly separated from him and crossed the sitting room, positioning herself beside the shrouded canvas. She cleared her throat. "Might I have your attention?"

The voices hushed.

"In celebration of family," she announced, "I would like to share with you all my latest work."

Flowers, he prayed. *Please be flowers.*

Without fanfare, Holly pulled the fabric off the canvas.

A tense energy filled the room. A silent, emotional

outburst.

Quincy had never sensed such a response, not from his kin or anyone else. Some were stone silent. Others gasped. Still others released soft sobs. What the devil was wrong? Or right? he wondered.

He searched the taut expressions of his brothers, his tearful sister. He couldn't understand what about the painting affected them in such a profound manner. Aye, the work was lovely, exceptionally lovely. A portrait of his sister and her infant son. Well, the babe had dark hair instead of his mother's golden curls, but the minor flaw would hardly cause such strain in the room, surely?

As the uneasy silence progressed, Quincy glanced at his wife. She twisted her fingers in expectation, and his heart pounded in sympathy with her. If so much as a negative word passed between a soul's lips, upsetting Holly . . .

"It's exquisite," whispered Mirabelle, finally releasing the pressure from the room. She turned toward James, her eyes overflowing with tears. "Is it like her?"

Quincy frowned. Her?

His eldest brother bobbed his head once, his expression still etched in stone. James then looked at William.

"Just like her," affirmed William, his voice unsteady.

Edmund walked up to the portrait and stroked its cheek in tender regard. "I can barely remember her."

"I have to thank James and William," said Holly, blushing with pleasure. "I could not have finished the piece without their vivid descriptions."

Quincy clearly wasn't part of his siblings shared experience *or* his wife's secret portrait. He glared at the painted face again, searching for the cryptic "her" everyone was talking about. He still saw Mirabelle, though. Aye, her brow was a tad wider. And the lines of her jaw were more narrow. Her chin had a dimple, but . . .

His heart seized. Breath trapped in his lungs. He suddenly recognized a woman he had never seen in his life.

Holly treaded back across the room. "Do you like it, Quincy?"

"Is that . . . ?"

She embraced him. "It's your Mother."

Quincy struggled against the tears welling in his throat. As he stared at the beautiful image of his mother, her eyes warm, so full of love for the babe in her arms, he trembled.

"She's holding you," continued Holly, her voice ever so tender.

He shook his head, resisting the inexplicable swelling in his breast. "That never happened," he rasped. "That moment never happened."

"It should have," returned James, voice brusque.

"Yes, it should have," affirmed Mirabelle.

His sister's umber eyes, still sparkling with tears, weakened him. He looked around the room, searching for the expressions of resentment he *knew* his siblings harbored for him, resentment for taking away their mother's life . . . but he saw none.

William eyed him with conviction. "She loved you, Quincy. She loved all of us."

The poignant sentiment, from the most reserved

of all his brothers, forced Quincy to take another look at the emotive artwork, and this time he allowed the inexplicable swelling in his breast to expand.

He glanced between the portrait of his mother and his wife and soon, unable to distinguish the love in their eyes for him, surrendered his guilt at last.

"Thank you," he breathed.

Her smile radiated. "You're welcome, husband."

"I think the evening's over," from James.

The family quietly vacated the sitting room, leaving the newlyweds in the intimate afterglow. The world seemed lighter, thought Quincy. Right. Balanced. And all because of Holly.

"I suppose we should retire, too," he murmured, stroking her spine in sensual caresses. "We have a wedding to attend in the morning."

As her smile broadened, she grasped his hand. "Come to bed, pirate."

And he followed her.

Most willingly.

Turn the page for a tantalizing preview of the next
book in The Hawkins Brothers series:

How to Steal a Pirate's Heart

Captain William Hawkins stood on the terrace outside his sister's fashionable townhouse in the heart of Mayfair. The noise and frippery inside the ballroom had triggered another throbbing headache, and he'd escaped the celebration in search of peace. The secluded garden, awash in milky moonlight, offered him tranquility, and he observed the gaiety through the glass terrace doors without feeling the disagreeable effects.

"There you are, Will."

His youngest brother, Quincy, stepped out onto the terrace, two crystal tumblers in hand.

The pup handed him a drink. "It's a brilliant affair, isn't it, Will? A celebration to remember for a hundred years. Amy looks prettier than a princess. And Eddie can't stop grinning. Can you believe it? Eddie!" He sighed. "They're finally going to be happy. It's about bloody time."

William watched the twirling newlyweds, both resplendent in their fancy duds. He shared Quincy's sentiment. His otherwise surly brother, Edmund, and his dashing bride, Lady Amy, had suffered enough hardship to last a lifetime.

"About time, indeed," said William. The twinge in his head worsened, and he clenched his eyes, grimacing.

"Are you all right?"

"Fine," he clipped. "It's just a headache."

"Tough luck, old fellow."

William snorted at the "old fellow" bit. At forty, he was seventeen years Quincy's senior, and ever since he'd reached the pinnacle year, his tactless brother had found it particularly amusing.

As music swelled into the night, Quincy remarked, "Belle really knows how to host a smashing reception."

After rubbing the bridge of his nose, William turned his gaze toward his sister, Mirabelle, the Duchess of Wembury. She was dancing with her husband, her cheeks flushed, so full of life. Two short years ago, she had almost died giving birth to her son. Even now, William's chest tightened at the agonizing memory.

As they had all learned at one time or another, life was precious, and momentous occasions needed to be marked with the proper fanfare—meaning food, drink and merrymaking galore.

A gust of laughter filled the terrace through the half open doors.

"Blimey," from Quincy. "Now that's a sound you don't hear every day."

William recognized the unusual merriment as belonging to his oldest brother, Captain James

Hawkins, the once infamous pirate Black Hawk. The man had the temperament of a raging bull, and his sudden, spirited outburst could only be ascribed to one source.

Sure enough, William located James with his exotic wife, Sophia, ensconced in a tête-à-tête near the ballroom doors. Whatever their exchange, it had amused the former corsair to no end.

The Hawkins family was happy. At last. Even the pup had much improved. A crippling melancholy had consumed him for years, but Quincy had also recently wed, his wife's healing touch having chased away his nightmares.

"A toast," said Quincy, raising his glass. "To happily-ever-after. Though late, 'tis better than never."

William offered a sardonic smile. Unlike the rest of his hard-drinking brothers, he never wallowed in alcohol. He didn't like to lose control of his senses. Ever. But more and more of late he'd made exceptions. He clinked his brother's glass before downing the fiery brandy.

Why not? thought William. After all, he was dying.

How to Steal a Pirate's Heart
COMING SOON!

WELCOME!

Enter the sensual and swashbuckling world of The Hawkins Brothers: four dark and dangerous pirates who retire their wicked ways after their sister becomes a duchess. But can the rugged rogues enter high society in Regency England, masquerading as gentlemen? Or will their true identities be revealed?

Learn all about the sexy brigands by turning the page, but beware! The Hawkins Brothers just might steal your heart and never give it back.

MY HERO

Take the following personality quiz and find out which Hawkins brother is best suited to steam up your night!

1. On a warm and sunny day, I'd be outside:
   A. On a nature walk
   B. Gardening
   C. Hosting a BBQ
   D. Playing sports

2. At a dinner party, I'm most likely to drink:
   A. Wine
   B. Ginger Ale
   C. Beer
   D. Anything!

3. My favorite holiday is:
   A. Valentine's Day
   B. Christmas
   C. Thanksgiving
   D. Halloween

4. If I could go anywhere in the world, I'd visit:
   A. Jamaica
   B. Africa
   C. Las Vegas
   D. Ibiza, Spain

5. My idea of the perfect date is:
   A. A late night picnic on the beach
   B. An intimate dinner at a restaurant
   C. Going to a football game
   D. An evening of dancing

ANSWERS: MY HERO

Mostly As: James Hawkins
Captain James Hawkins, the infamous pirate leader Black Hawk, is the oldest of the Hawkins brood and wields the greatest brute strength. As the head of the family, he is saddled with responsibility and can prove stubborn at times as he struggles to keep his kin together and away from the gallows. He prizes loyalty above all other qualities and possesses a lusty appetite for life's simple pleasures. A true alpha male, he can communicate an order to a tar (or a desire to a woman) with just one piercing look. However, he also has a tender side, achingly soft at times, but well concealed. It is only in moments of great peace that he drops his iron front and lets the tenderness show.

See James Hawkins meet his match in *The Infamous Rogue* and *Mistress of Paradise*.

Mostly Bs: William Hawkins
William Hawkins is the second eldest and the most levelheaded of the Hawkins brood. Intelligent and even tempered, he can see both sides of a story clearly. He has a knack for settling a conflict before it gets out of hand, earning him the status of peacemaker in the tempestuous family. But William's sensibility leads to emotional indifference, making him a stranger to romantic love. Will the responsible William open his heart at last, and let the wild and stormy ways of love take root?

Find out in *How to Steal a Pirate's Heart (Coming Soon)*.

Mostly Cs: Edmund Hawkins

Hot-tempered Edmund Hawkins is the middle brother. He enjoys a big meal and a good round of fisticuffs. Secretive, he tends to keep to himself, talking only if he has something worthwhile to impart. He is content to let his older brothers rule the roost, while he searches for amusement elsewhere ... in London's underworld. Will the brooding Edmund find a woman who will bring out the champion in him?

Look for his emotional story in *The Notorious Scoundrel*.

Mostly Ds: Quincy Hawkins

The pup, Quincy Hawkins, is the youngest of the Hawkins brood and the most likely to get into scrapes. Charming and flirtatious, he makes the ladies swoon. He's always ready for fun or adventure—even if it lands him in the gaol. He's honest (too honest) and will always tell you what's on his mind. But the fun-loving rake possesses another, darker side. Personal demons lead him astray. Will he find a deep and enduring love to help him reconcile with his tortured past?

Don't miss his tale in *How to Seduce a Pirate*.

THE HAWKINS BROTHERS SERIES

Mistress of Paradise (prequel):
A dark and troubled soul, Captain James Hawkins seeks freedom from his tortured past as the infamous pirate, Black Hawk. But when he meets a seductive beauty on the island of Jamaica, he finds a passion greater than any foray at sea.

Sassy, fierce and independent, Sophia Dawson knows her heart's desire — and it's the sexy brigand who tempts her with promises of pleasure. In his arms she finds erotic delight and respite from duty as her mad father's caretaker.

But a storm lurks on the horizon as the couple's heated affair attracts scorn from the islanders. Will James and Sophia weather the brutal tempest . . . or will there be trouble in paradise?

To see if James and Sophia find love in each other's arms again, read their story in *The Infamous Rogue*, available now from Avon Books.

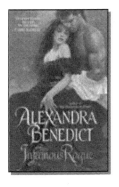

The Infamous Rogue (book one):
The daughter of a wealthy bandit, Sophia Dawson once lost herself in the arms of Black Hawk, the most infamous pirate ever to command the high seas. But now, determined to put her sinful past behind her, she prepares to enter society as the bride of a well-born nobleman who knows nothing of her scandalous youth. All goes according to plan until her ex-lover — now a respectable sea captain but just as handsome and dangerous as ever — appears and once again tempts her with desire.

From the moment he sees Sophia again, James Hawkins wants only one thing: revenge. He'll see to it that the reckless beauty pays for abandoning their heated affair. And so begins a battle of wills that can end only in utter ruin . . . or wicked surrender . . .

"The sexy, intriguing pirates Benedict introduced in Too Great a Temptation return as the heroes of their own series. But men like these need heroines to match, and Benedict has created a smart and sassy spitfire of a woman to add spice and heat to a tale filled with biting repartee and passionate drama. You'll relish this lively high-seas romp."

Romantic Times Book Reviews
on *The Infamous Rogue*, Also a Reviewer's Choice
Nominee for Best Historical Romantic Adventure

The Notorious Scoundrel (book two):

Like an irresistible siren, the veiled dancer with the bewitching green eyes lures dukes and earls into London's underworld to see her dance – and succumb to her spell. Some says she's a princess, but only one man knows her darkest secret.

She is Amy Peel, an orphan from the city's rookeries, and she believes the bold rogue who unmasks her to be nothing but a scoundrel – albeit a dangerously handsome one. He may have rescued her from an attempted kidnapping, but she will not give in to his sensual seduction or to the wicked desire she begins to feel . . .

He is Edmund Hawkins, swashbuckling pirate turned reluctant gentleman, and he will not let the lovely Amy slip through his grasp, especially when he learns she's in greater peril than she could possibly know. He will do everything in his power to protect her – for this notorious scoundrel has truly, unbelievably, lost his heart . . .

"The sexy, dashing Hawkins brothers return, lifting readers' hearts and temperatures. Benedict employs intense emotions, a keen awareness of human nature and sensuality to enhance stories filled with action and adventure, unforgettable characters and unique plotlines."

Romantic Times Book Reviews,
Top Pick! review of *The Notorious Scoundrel*

How to Seduce a Pirate (book three):

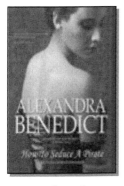

The downtrodden daughter of a viscount, the Honorable Miss Holly Turner is desperate for money and assumes the secret identity of Lord H — the erotic artist — but her carefully crafted world turns on its ear when she stumbles into the room of one very handsome — and very naked — gentleman, mistaking him for her model.

Quincy Hawkins is chasing the dragon, hoping to outrun the demons from his past, but when an audacious — albeit beautiful — wench paints him in the buff, mayhem erupts. What is a gentleman pirate to do when scandal strikes? Marry the wench, of course. There's just one hitch. He won't bed her. Ever. His charming wife has already stolen from him his likeness, his freedom, and Quincy won't give her anything more . . . not even his body.

Holly can't believe her ears. A marriage in name alone? She will never have a wedding night? She will never know the pleasure of her husband's sensuous touch? Well, she won't stand for it. She intends to have a real marriage — with all the sensual benefits — even if it means seducing her stubborn pirate.

And don't miss *Too Great a Temptation* and *Too Dangerous to Desire* where The Hawkins Brothers first appeared as supporting characters — and stole readers' hearts!

Too Great a Temptation:
A lord so sinful he is dubbed the "Duke of Rogues," Damian Westmore lives for pleasure — until the day his brother dies at the hands of pirates. Abandoning the libertine life to pursue revenge, Damian finds the criminals he seeks and joins their crew in disguise, waiting for the chance to strike the brigands down. But he never imagined there would be a woman on board — or that the stunning siren would inflame the very passions Damian swore to resist until his brother's death was avenged.

Beautiful, fiery Mirabelle Hawkins longs for the freedom of the high seas — so she stows away on her brother's pirate ship at the first opportunity. But she finds something more exciting than chase and plunder: a bold, handsome, secretive sailor whose touch makes her tremble with desire . . . but whose love is a cutlass that could destroy all she holds dear.

"Fans of historical romance will thoroughly enjoy this fresh take on the genre."

Publisher's Weekly,
Starred Review of *Too Great a Temptation*

Too Dangerous to Desire:

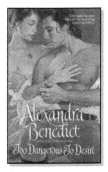

Lonely and overcome with grief after a painful loss in his past, Adam Westmore walks the ocean's edge in solitude.

Forced to marry a depraved foreign prince, Evelyn Waye believes she has no choice but to throw herself from the jagged cliffs into the crashing surf below.

When Adam sees the enchanting woman in terrible danger, he rescues her from death and brings her back to his humble cottage. Hesitant to reveal his true identity as a distinguished lord, he nonetheless offers to protect her. And she needs protection, for the prince will find her — and harm her.

Evelyn wants to trust the handsome stranger who saved her life, but her cursed beauty has made her suspicious of all men . . . even one whose kindness disarms her, whose gentle touch inspires passion within her.

Soon Adam and Evelyn are consumed by desire . . . a dangerous desire that puts their very lives in peril.

"An outstanding read."

Romance Reader at Heart,
Top Pick! review of *Too Dangerous to Desire*

ABOUT THE AUTHOR

Alexandra Benedict is the author of several historical romances published by Avon Books. She also writes fiction as an Indie Author. Her work has received critical acclaim from *Booklist* and a starred review from *Publishers Weekly*. All of her books are translated into various languages. For more information visit:

www.AlexandraBenedict.ca

54786262R00115

Made in the USA
Lexington, KY
28 August 2016